Anne lost her balance and was about to fall . . .

Rob's hand shot out and grabbed her arm, and she instinctively clutched at him, steadying herself. "That was close," she murmured, her lashes dropping to her cheeks.

Yes, he was close, too close. She could smell his damp skin, feel it where her fingers curled over his arm. Instead of pushing herself away, she turned her gaze up to him. He was looking at her through narrowed eyes, eyes that flashed briefly as his nostrils flared and his firm lips parted. For a moment, she thought his lips would descend to claim hers . . . and then he moved away.

"Thanks for the use of the pool," he said impersonally as he picked up his T-shirt. And with a curt little nod, he headed out of the yard.

"Goodbye to you, too," Anne whispered in dismay.

SAMANTHA DAY, a Canadian author, used to work in a school library but now makes romance writing her full-time occupation. Having perfected the art of daydreaming, she says she learned how to transcribe what she saw in her mind onto sheets of blank paper. Her husband and daughter are wonderfully supportive and encouraging of her romance writing.

Books by Samantha Day

HARLEQUIN ROMANCE

2672—THE TURN OF THE TIDE
2840—FOR KARIN'S SAKE
2923—THERE MUST BE LOVE

UNDER A SUMMER SUN

Samantha Day

Harlequin Books

TORONTO • NEW YORK • LONDON
AMSTERDAM • PARIS • SYDNEY • HAMBURG
STOCKHOLM • ATHENS • TOKYO • MILAN

ISBN 0-373-03015-0

Harlequin Romance first edition November 1989

Printed in U.S.A.

CHAPTER ONE

"SO, HOW WAS IT?" Margo Hammond looked at her sister-in-law, a bemused expression in her soft brown eyes.

"Wonderful." Anne pulled a stool from the breakfast counter and sat down, wrapping her legs around the rungs as she leaned forward. "It was beautiful. The stars were so incredibly bright and the coyotes sang for me all night long. I didn't get much sleep, but it was worth it."

"I still think you're nuts," Margo said mildly as she took plates from the dishwasher and stacked them in the cupboard. "Home one night, then off camping all by yourself the next." She shook her head. "Why anyone would want to spend the night sleeping on the ground—the cold, hard ground—with all kinds of *things* creeping around is beyond me."

"It's great," Anne said with a laugh. "It soothes the soul. You don't know what you're missing."

"Oh, yes, I do. That brother of yours dragged me out camping a few times, until he realized I wasn't about to be converted. Now he takes the boys and leaves me to my creature comforts—a soft bed, indoor plumbing and—" she put two mugs onto the countertop "—coffee minus the layer of ashes it gets after being boiled over a campfire for hours." She poured fragrant coffee into the mugs and slid one across the counter to Anne.

"Philistine," Anne accused with a grin.

"Darned right." Margo sat down opposite Anne and took a sip of her coffee, sighing with pleasure. "What are you up to today?"

"I'm going to help you get ready for the party tonight."

Margo shook her head quickly. "Everything is under control. You can just sit by the pool and relax."

"I don't need to relax, Margo," Anne protested. "Really."

"Well, if I'd just spent four days towing a trailer full of furniture fifteen hundred miles across the country and last night sleeping on a rock, *I'd* need to relax. So you'd better—I want you in top form tonight, not yawning in some corner."

"I promise not to yawn. Who's coming to this party, anyway?"

"The usual bunch—who else is there? People move away from here, not to. Oh—but there is Rob MacNeil, the man who bought the land from your dad. He might show up. At least, Ken invited him, but he's inclined to keep to himself."

Anne looked down at her mug, rubbing a finger around the rim. She had hoped to own that land someday. Not all of it, just the one little corner overlooking the river. She had assumed it would always be there waiting for her when she decided to move back to Manitoba. She felt a strong sense of regret that her father had had to sell the land he loved but could no longer afford to farm. Now it belonged to a stranger.

"What's he like?" she asked Margo, looking up.

"Rob? Pure unadulterated hunk!" Margo said unexpectedly, a gleam of appreciation in her eyes. "Tall—taller than Ken. With shoulders out to here." She held out her hands. "And the most striking eyes—somewhere between brown and gold. Like topaz."

"Does Ken know?"

Margo blinked at her, puzzled. "Know what?"

Anne's blue eyes sparkled with laughter. "That he's got a rival."

Margo gave a little snort of laughter. "I'm married, not buried, Annie. I can look, can't I?"

"I suppose," Anne said, laughing. "Tell me, while you were doing all this looking, did you discover a personality, or is he just a lot of brawn?"

"I can't say I know him all that well," Margo admitted. "Ken and your dad have spent a fair bit of time with him, and the boys, too. They all seem to like him. I tried to get Ken to dig for details about his personal life, but you know your brother. He has absolutely no urge to gossip." She made a little face.

"Your mom hasn't had much luck with your dad, either. He and Ken are a lot alike that way, aren't they? But I do know he isn't married." She studied Anne, her eyes taking on a thoughtful gleam.

Anne caught the look and shook her head quickly, holding up her hands in protest. "Uh-uh. No way. Forget it, Margo. No matchmaking. I'm just not ready to become involved with anyone, and even if I was, I wouldn't want my family setting me up with the man next door."

"I guess it could get embarrassing," Margo admitted with a laugh. "Anyway, the last time I heard anything about your love life, you were seeing someone—Graham?''

''Graham,'' Anne confirmed, frowning at the memory.

Margo looked at her closely for a moment. ''I got the impression it was on the serious side. What happened?''

''Another woman. Or, more accurately, other women.'' Anne's eyes clouded briefly. ''He was a very attractive man, Margo, and he knew it. Reveled in it,'' she added with a grimace, remembering how his conceit had gradually revealed itself to her. ''Once I'd gotten over the shock of finding out I wasn't the love of his life—at least, not in the way I wanted to be—I realized I didn't like him very much. Not really.'' She gave a self-deprecating shrug. ''I was in too much of a hurry, I guess. I was getting to the point in my life where I really wanted to meet someone special. I should have seen Graham for what he really was—shallow and self-absorbed.''

''I'm sorry, Anne.'' Margo's voice was softly sympathetic.

Anne shook her head. ''Don't be. Finding out he wasn't faithful just didn't hurt the way it should have if I'd really loved him. I was attracted to him, yes, but it was nothing that would have lasted. I was lucky to find that out before things went any further.''

''Was breaking up with Graham why you decided to move back?''

Anne tapped a finger on the edge of the counter, finding it easy to slip back into the old habit of confiding in her sister-in-law. ''It's part of the reason,'' she confessed. ''But basically it was time for a change.

And I realized one day that—well, home won't always be here. Mom and Dad aren't getting any younger, and the boys will be out on their own before much longer." She smiled at Margo. "I guess I just wanted to come home while I still could."

Margo nodded, understanding what Anne was saying. "How did Graham take it—or did you tell him?"

"I told him." Anne's smile twisted as she remembered how he'd insisted on seeing her after she'd told him things were over; how smugly confident he'd been that he could win her back. "He couldn't understand why I wouldn't forgive him 'for being a man,' to use his words. Or why I'd give up the bright lights of Toronto and the glamour of modeling to teach in some 'backwoods prairie school,' his words again."

"I must admit, I have a bit of trouble with that myself," Margo said. "Maybe a nice long holiday back here was all you needed."

"No," Anne said with conviction. "Not this time. I spent over ten years in Toronto," she explained. "Bright lights fade into the background after a while. And as far as the modeling went—" she gave a little laugh and shook her head "—I never did get into the glamour part of it. Believe me, posing endlessly for catalog layouts and department-store flyers isn't glamorous. Maybe if I'd been a top-line model it might have been different, but as it was, it was a basically boring job that paid the bills while I went to university." She grinned suddenly. "Mundane as it sounds, all I ever wanted to do was teach."

"History," Margo said with a grimace.

"Canadian history," Anne clarified with a laugh. "Now there must be something I can do to help you get ready for tonight."

"Well, if you insist—"

"I do."

"Then you can pick the strawberries. I'm going to serve them with whipped cream and the ladyfingers I made last night while you were out howling at the moon or whatever it was you were up to."

"There was no moon and I didn't howl. Although I was tempted to join in with the coyotes the way Ken and I did when we were kids."

"You're both loony," Margo muttered, handing Anne a large enameled bowl for the strawberries.

"And you love it," Anne teased, taking the bowl. "Fill 'er up?"

"As many as you can. What we don't use tonight, I'll freeze."

OUTSIDE, the sun was hot in a clear blue sky. Anne walked under elm trees spreading dappled shade onto the lawn, which sloped down to a tiny stream. The air was sweetly perfumed by the abundant rosebushes her mother had planted when she had first arrived from England, a war bride overawed by the immensity of the land that was to be her new home.

The scent of roses always made Anne think of her mother, and she smiled as she approached the patch of strawberries, wondering how her parents were enjoying their extended visit to England. She had seen them briefly in May, when they had stopped in Toronto en route. They had been thrilled to learn she would be moving back to Manitoba and would be teaching in the regional high school come September.

Anne crouched between the two rows of strawberry plants, putting the bowl down in front of her. She brushed aside the deep green leaves to expose the berries beneath, snipping them from the vine with her thumbnail. She ate the first few sun-warm berries, savoring the sweet bite of juice against her tongue as she recalled her mother admonishing her as a child not to eat more than she picked. Popping in one last berry, she began to pick in earnest, working her way down the long rows.

When she reached the end, the bowl was full, and she stood, grimacing as her knees creaked in protest. After stretching the kinks from her back, she picked up the bowl and headed back to the house.

The building was an interesting combination of old and new. Rather than have a new one built when he married Margo, Ken had added a wing to his parents' house, giving him and his bride private quarters under the same roof. The single-story addition ambled out from the south side of the older house. With the surrounding lawns and bright flower beds, it was all very attractive, and Anne looked around with a rush of pleasure, struck again by how right the sense of coming home was.

"BACK ON THE FARM for two days and already you're hard at work."

Anne turned from the sink, where she was hulling strawberries, to smile warmly at her brother as he stood in the doorway. The lines around his blue eyes crinkled as he returned her smile.

"I don't consider it work when the result is something good to eat. Aren't you home early?" she asked, glancing at the clock on the wall.

"I had a couple of hours owing for some overtime," Ken answered. "I thought I'd get an early start on the weekend and," he added, his voice deep with pleasure, "my holidays."

Anne looked at Ken's sweat-stained shirt. "Work hard today?"

"Yeah—and the heat made it worse." Ken opened the fridge door and took out a canned drink. Popping the top, he raised the can to his lips and took a long swallow, then sighed with satisfaction as he put it down. "The thought of a cold drink and a swim was all that kept me going."

"A swim sounds great," Anne said. "I've got a couple of kinks from sleeping on the ground last night that need working out."

"Enjoyed the camp-out, did you?"

"It was great, Ken. You don't know how much I've missed doing things like that."

"I know how much I'd miss it. Ready for that swim?"

"Just let me finish these last few strawberries. I wanted to get them done before Margo did."

"Speaking of Margo, where is she?"

"Lying down, resting up for the party tonight."

Ken nodded. "Good. She always knocks herself out getting ready for these things. I keep telling her nobody would care if all they got was hamburgers and potato chips."

"Margo would," Anne said with a laugh. She pulled the hulls from the last of the berries and left the fruit in a colander to drain. "How about that swim, big brother?"

"You got it, li'l sis. Let's get in there before the boys get home from school and turn the place into a war zone."

The pool was a recent addition, put in after Alan Hammond had sold the land he'd farmed for over fifty years, land left to him by his father and land he had fully expected to leave to his son. Anne had hated to see it go, but she understood the immense strain her father and brother had been under trying to earn a decent living by farming. And while she might resent the fact that it had to be so, it was a relief to see Ken and Margo so relaxed and happy, to know her parents could enjoy a comfortable retirement. The sale of the land hadn't made them rich, but the financial pressures were gone. Ken now worked for the provincial government as an attendant for Spruce Woods Park, a job that kept him in the outdoors he loved and provided him with a steady wage for the first time in his life, as well as the promise of a decent pension when he retired.

They were luckier than many farm families. At least they had been able to retain ownership of the house and ten acres surrounding it. That was some consolation, Anne reflected, dangling her feet in the turquoise water.

Ken's head shot out of the water, by her feet, and he grinned at her as he wiped a hand across his face.

"Have you got any regrets, Ken?" she asked as he pulled himself out of the pool to sit beside her. "About selling the land?"

"About selling the land—of course. About not farming anymore—definitely not."

"I always thought you liked farming."

"I did." He shook moisture from his thick blond hair. "I never minded the hours or the work. I just couldn't take any more of the uncertainty, the things I had no control over—weather, falling grain prices. Combine that with the fact that we needed to start replacing equipment..." He shook his head. "It was time to quit. Besides, I like what I'm doing now, and the regular hours and paychecks aren't bad, either. I can finally afford to take Margo on that honeymoon we missed out on seventeen years ago."

"Six weeks in Europe. It sounds great, Ken."

"It will be," he said confidently. "And Anne, thanks for offering to take care of the boys until they go to Margo's parents. I want you to know we appreciate it."

"I'm looking forward to it. I've hardly seen them since they were toddlers. This'll give us a chance to get to know each other all over again. It'll be a fun three weeks."

"Yeah, well..." Ken frowned. "Scott's a good kid, but Steve—lately there are times I could wring his neck."

Anne gave a little laugh. "He's sixteen—it's normal. Give him a year or two and he'll turn human again. Just in time for Scott to start acting up."

"Well, anyway, I hope he listens to you. Just in case, I asked Rob MacNeil to keep an eye on things, to give you a hand." Ken glanced sideways at her. "He's the guy who—"

"Bought the land. Yeah, I know. Margo told me." Anne frowned at her brother. "You didn't need to go to him, Ken. I'm all grown up now. I can take care of things on my own. I won't feel comfortable with some stranger poking around."

"He's an okay guy, Annie. And it'll make me feel better knowing he's around to help out."

"Always the big brother," Anne said, sighing. She'd let the matter drop as far as Ken was concerned, but she silently vowed she wouldn't tolerate any interference, especially from a man she didn't even know.

"By the way, Rob comes by to use the pool now and then. It's kind of an exchange—he's got a couple of horses he lets Scott and me ride whenever we want. Beautiful animals," Ken continued, his blue eyes gleaming with appreciation, "Arabians. I'm sure there'd be no problem if you wanted to ride."

It had been years since Anne had been on horseback and the thought of riding again held a definite appeal. "Does he breed them?" she asked curiously.

"He's just getting started, but it's a good line." Ken looked a bit envious. "It'd be great to have the money to get into something like that. He's turned the fields into pasture. Grows hay, oats, some alfalfa. It's doing pretty good."

"Did he farm before moving here?"

Ken shook his head. "He had a partnership in an advertising firm. Sold out a couple of years ago, he told me. I understand he made quite a profit. Got himself set up comfortably. I know he didn't have to ask the bank for a mortgage, and he gave us what we were asking."

Anne had to admire Ken's attitude. He was still keenly aware of the land he had worked for so many years, but seemed to harbor no resentment toward the man who could so easily afford to buy it and run it to indulge himself with expensive hobbies.

"Where did he build his house?" she asked.

"On the bluff overlooking the river. You know, the place where we used to camp when we were kids. You'll love it, Annie," he went on enthusiastically. "He did a good job planning it. The house blends in with the trees and the roll of the land, all weathered wood and glass. Modern, but not out of place."

Anne looked down into the water, kicking a heel against the side of the pool, feeling a strong regret that that favorite piece of land was lost to her forever. It was in that spot that she'd hoped to build a home for herself someday.

"Annie—"

She looked at Ken. "What?"

"I just want you to know that—well, I'm glad you're back," he said with gruff affection.

"Me, too," Anne responded with a warm smile. "Even if it means being bossed around by my big brother all over again." She punched playfully at his arm.

"Hey, watch it," Ken growled. "Don't get uppity." He put his hands on her back and pushed her into the water.

Anne came up sputtering and laughing. Bringing her hands down sharply, she sent a spray of water into Ken's face, then swam quickly to the other side of the pool and hauled herself out before he could retaliate.

"See you later, big brother," she called, grinning widely. Scooping up her towel, she patted her face dry as she headed to the house.

Anne had taken over her old bedroom in her parents' section of the big house. The room hadn't changed much since her high-school days. The posters and pictures were gone, but the rose-sprigged wallpaper and crisp, ruffled curtains were the same. She pushed back the curtains and sat on the cushioned window seat with her legs tucked under her, as she had done countless times in the past. Plans had been made here; dreams had come and gone. She rested her forehead against the glass, a warm breeze caressing her face as she breathed deeply the late-spring scent of green growth.

It is good to be back, she thought. Her years away had been, for the most part, wonderful, a time of great personal growth and achievement, but Manitoba had always felt like home. Her stay in Toronto, extended as it had been, had always seemed temporary.

She'd gone to Toronto fresh out of school to attend university while she lived with her father's younger sister, Frances. Anne had been a rather gawky, self-conscious teenager, uncomfortable in the body that had grown seemingly overnight. Her aunt Fran, wanting to do something special for her only niece, enrolled her in a modeling school, hoping to build Anne's confidence. Anne learned the art of applying makeup and how to choose the clothes that best suited her. As her confidence grew, her poise increased and the results were astonishing.

The makeup emphasized her wide, smoky-blue eyes, giving them a sultry look. Her high cheekbones were accented, as were her full, slightly pouting lips. Sun-streaked hair the color of wheat tumbled down her back in deep, shining waves. As her posture improved, Anne no longer felt her five feet ten inches to be too tall, her nicely curved body too big. For the first time it all seemed to fit, and the awkward teenager became an attractive, self-assured young woman. When she was offered a chance to do some modeling, she jumped at it. While it might not have been her first career choice, it did pay enough that she could attend her university classes without the pressure of financial worries.

Guided by her sensible aunt, Anne did not get caught up in the thrill of superficial glamour. Thanks to Frances, she never lost sight of her childhood goal: becoming a teacher. Frances helped her to realize that modeling was a short-lived career at best. Teaching, helping the history of her country to come alive to children, would give her satisfaction for years to come.

Resting her back against the wall of the window seat, Anne stretched her legs out in front of her, smiling at the memory of that shy and insecure teenager. The insecurity had long since vanished and the shyness was hidden under a hard-won layer of self-confidence.

Anne had been careful about her decision to move back to Manitoba. Once she'd received her master's degree and had a couple of years' teaching experience, there seemed little point in continuing to live in Toronto. Her aunt had married and was deeply involved with her husband, and there was no one else to keep her there.

Especially not Graham, Anne thought, wrinkling her nose.

There was still a little corner of her heart that regretted their relationship had had to end. At twenty-nine, she had reached a time in her life when she had really wanted to be loved and cherished by a special man. It had seemed for a while as though Graham were that man.

Maybe it's just as well he wasn't faithful, Anne reflected, staring broodingly out the window. She had to admit to herself that once she got past the initial attraction she felt toward him, they really had little in common. Marriage to him would have been a disaster. There had been no real substance to their relationship, nothing that would have endured the passage of time. But, blinded by her attraction to him, charmed by his good looks and the fun he had initially offered, she hadn't seen that he wasn't the man for her.

Had she deluded herself that she felt more than just a physical attraction because she was at a point where she really wanted marriage and a family? She had become very aware that her time for bearing children was running out, and subconsciously that must have affected her feelings, blinding her to Graham's true character.

If she hadn't caught him in a lie and realized that she wasn't the only woman in his life and undoubtedly never would be, she might have gone so far as to marry him. He had wanted it. Anne had come to understand that it was enough for him that they looked the ideal couple. It would never have done for her.

Somewhere out there, Anne knew, was the right man for her, and if he was a long time in coming, then so be it. Maybe, she reflected, she'd be like Aunt Fran. Fran had been alone a long time, but when she met Hugh, the spark, the magic were there. Even Anne could see it, and she rejoiced in her aunt's happiness.

I'll just have to be a little more careful next time, Anne thought, resolving to have her eyes wide open before she went into another relationship.

There was a tap on her door as it was pushed open. "Anne?"

Anne looked away from the window to see Margo. "Hi, come in."

Margo came into the room and flopped down on the bed, stretching with a wide yawn. "That's the trouble with afternoon naps," she said with another stretch. "They never seem long enough. I always feel more tired after than before." She rolled over onto her side, propping her head on her hand. "So, what are you wearing tonight?"

Anne shrugged. "Shorts, I guess. With my bathing suit underneath. We will be swimming, won't we?"

"Probably. But Anne..." Margo gave a little grimace and sat up. "Wear something a little more glamorous than shorts, will you? I mean, you look great in them with those long legs of yours, but—well, I think everyone would like to see a little bit of the big-city model."

Anne groaned and shook her head. "Come on, Margo. No way. That part of me is finished. From now on I'm just plain, ordinary me."

Margo looked at her sister-in-law and gave a little hoot of laughter. "Plain and ordinary you? Tell me another one. Look, I'm not asking you to go around striking poses all night long. It's just that people here would get a kick out of seeing you glammed up a bit."

"I don't see why," Anne said, frowning. "I mean, they've known me all my life. Half of them came to visit me when I was in Toronto. What difference is it going to make to anyone whether I wear shorts tonight?"

"It'll make a difference to me," Margo said. "Come on, open up your closet and show me what you've got."

With an obliging sigh, Anne went to the closet and opened the door. "There. Skirts, slacks and blouses. What'd you expect?" she said in answer to Margo's look of disappointment. "I'm a teacher."

Margo pushed through the clothes. "What about this?" she asked, puling out a skirt Anne had bought while on holiday in Hawaii. It was whirls of pink and burgundy on a black background and was made to be worn over a bathing suit, it tied over one hip, leaving a long slit up the thigh.

"It's perfect for a poolside party," Margo said with satisfaction as she laid it on the bed. "Have you got a bathing suit that'll go with it?"

Resigned, Anne pulled open a dresser drawer and took out a black strapless suit. "This one."

"Perfect. Now—your hair."

"I was going to pull it back in a French braid. I suppose that's not good enough, either."

"It depends. Are you going swimming?"

"Probably."

"Then the braid is best. It looks good and won't be ruined by the water."

"I'm glad I can do something right," Anne muttered.

Margo grinned. "One more thing."

"Of course."

"Put on a bit more makeup than you usually do—especially around the eyes. Waterproof."

"Yes, Boss. Anything else?"

"Just be yourself."

"If I was going to be myself, I'd be wearing shorts." Anne sat at her dresser and looked into the mirror. Picking up a comb, she dragged it through hair still damp from the shower she had taken after her swim with Ken, then deftly began to braid it. When she had finished, she pulled at a few short strands until they curled softly around her face.

"Good enough?" she asked Margo, who was sitting cross-legged on the edge of the bed, watching her.

Margo nodded. "Now the makeup."

Anne glanced at the clock beside the bed. "There's lots of time yet. Nobody'll be here for a couple of hours."

"I just want to make sure you do it right." Margo leaned forward, her elbows resting on her knees. "Come on, Annie. Gild the lily."

Anne gave her sister-in-law a look of exasperation. "Since when have you become so bossy? I've got to have a talk with my brother—he must be slipping somewhere." As she reached for her makeup bag, she turned and looked at Margo with sudden suspicion. "What's behind all this, anyway? Something tells me you're up to something."

Margo's eyes widened with hurt innocence. "Who, me?" She shook her dark, curly hair. "It's just kind of nice to do sister things again, the way we did before you moved away. It's fun to talk about clothes and makeup...men..."

"Well, it'll have to be clothes and makeup, because there are no men in my life and I know all about the one in yours." Anne started to apply eye shadow, remembering how close she and Margo had become after Margo's marriage to Ken. She'd been just like an older sister, easy to confide in, accepting and not inclined to lecture. Their relationship had remained close over the years in spite of the distance separating them. There had been many late-night telephone conversations and lots of long letters. As far as Anne was concerned, her brother couldn't have married anyone better, and she was glad to see the marriage still seemed solid and loving.

"Nice," Margo said approvingly as Anne finished off her eye makeup with a coat of mascara. "You have the prettiest eyes, a lot like Ken's. And Steven's."

"Steven's really beginning to look like Ken. He's already nearly as tall." She carefully dusted blush onto her cheeks.

"But he's not much like him in temperament," Margo said, making a little face. "That boy is pretty growly these days. And it isn't helping that Ken said he couldn't get his driver's license until we got back from Europe. It seems mean to him, I know, but we thought it would make things easier for you. It's hard enough to keep track of him these days without him driving off somewhere."

She watched Anne apply lip gloss. "I'm glad you're here to take care of them, Anne. We were going to send them to Brandon to stay with my parents for the whole six weeks at first, but I think it would have been too hard on Mom. Scotty, okay—but not Steven." She shook her head, looking far too young to be the mother of a sixteen-year-old boy. "I sure hope he grows out of it soon. I also hope you're not going to have all sorts of trouble with him."

"I don't think so," Anne said confidently. "Steven and I have always gotten along great."

"Yes, but..." Margo sighed. "He's changed a lot in the past few months."

"He's just testing his limits," Anne assured her. "As he should be doing at his age. And kids are never as bad with other people as they are with their parents. It'll do all of you good to be away from one another for a while. The main thing is that you and Ken get all you can from this trip and not worry about what's happening here." Anne grinned as she turned away from the mirror. "I'm a high-school teacher, remember? I can handle teenagers."

"I suppose so..."

"Don't suppose—know it. It's only for three weeks, anyway. And by the time I ship them off to your parents, they'll be too exhausted to get up to much. I've got plans for those strapping lads of yours. Gramma's house needs scrubbing from top to bottom—and painting—before I move in. And I don't plan on doing it all myself."

"So you're definite about moving into the old house."

"Absolutely." The original farmhouse still stood, only a few hundred feet from the house Anne's father built when he'd returned from the war with his bride. It was small, not much more than a cottage, but it was cozy and in good repair in spite of having been closed up since her grandmother's death nearly four years ago.

"You know you could stay here," Margo ventured.

"I know. But I've been on my own for a long time now. I like it. And besides, you know Mother. If I'm under her roof, she'll be fussing over me like a mother hen."

"It might not be so bad," Margo said with a laugh. "Her fussing is split a lot of ways now, between your dad, Ken and the boys."

"Haven't you found it a bit hard, sharing a house all these years?"

Margo shook her head quickly. "It's been great, actually. Especially when the boys were little. Besides, the way this place is built, we have a lot of privacy. Your mom really respects that. And," she added with a grin, "we're able to share a kitchen quite easily. I like to cook—she likes to bake." Margo unfolded her legs and stood. "Speaking of kitchens, I've got a couple of things to finish up. I guess I should get started."

"Anything I can do to help?"

"Not just yet. I'll make use of you later, though," she promised as she pushed open the door.

"Just see that you do," Anne said, picking up the skirt from the bed and shaking it out. "By the way, what are *you* wearing?"

Margo stuck her head back through the doorway and grinned. "Shorts," she said, and shut the door with a little wave.

The skirt with the strapless black bathing suit suited Anne's tall, curvy figure perfectly. As she moved, a flash of long golden leg was visible through the slit in the side of the skirt. Her thick rope of blond hair swayed gently against her bare, tanned back, while her eyes glowed a sultry blue above well-defined cheekbones. Anne smoothed the skirt over her hips, slid her feet into flat, strappy sandals and left her room for the kitchen.

Her younger nephew, Scott, was there drinking a glass of milk.

"Hi, Annie," he said with his sweet, almost shy smile. His hair and eyes were dark like his mother's, but at twelve he already showed signs of having his father's height.

"Hi, Scotty." Anne smiled with affection. "How was school today?"

He shrugged. "Okay, I guess. We're not really busy anymore—we're supposed to be studying for exams."

"And are you?" Anne opened the fridge door and took out a pitcher of orange juice, pouring herself a glass.

"I know it all already," Scott replied confidently.

"Yeah," said Steven, coming into the kitchen. "He thinks he's a real brain or something."

"At least I'm not a meathead like you," Scott retorted quickly.

Anne gave her head a little shake and smiled at the two boys. "It's so nice to see you two getting along so well. I was worried you'd do nothing but fight while your parents were away."

"I don't fight," Scott said. "He does."

Before Steven could answer, their mother came into the kitchen. "From where I stand, you're both just as bad. Try to tone it down, before you scare your aunt away, okay, guys? Try not to give her a hard time."

"I won't," Scott said quickly. "I'll just ignore him." He jabbed his thumb at his brother.

"Jerk," Steven muttered, opening the fridge door to peer inside.

"Jock," Scott jeered.

Margo sighed. "Forget the name-calling, guys. Steven, you're to finish mowing the lawn before you do anything else. Scott, I want you to be sure the pool is clean before your dad drops you off at the Wilsons'. Did you remember to pack your toothbrush this time?"

"Yeah, I think so."

"Well, check before you leave, okay? And remember to thank Mrs. Wilson for having you tonight. Steven, what are your plans?"

Steven emerged from behind the fridge door with an apple in his hand. "Baseball. Brad's picking me up." He took a big bite of the apple.

"And after?"

"I dunno," he mumbled, his mouth full. "Go to Bud's Drive-In for a hamburger, I guess."

"No drinking, Steven," his mother said quietly, looking as though she wanted to say more.

"Aw, Mom. I said I wouldn't, didn't I?" Steven growled as he shut the fridge door with his foot. "I gotta go cut the grass." He left the room quickly.

Margo sighed as she watched her elder son leave. Turning to Scott, she ruffled the dark curls that were so like her own. "Get the pool done, okay, Scotty?"

"Sure, Mom." With a willing smile, Scott left through the kitchen door.

"Who's this Brad?" Anne asked as soon as he had gone.

"Brad Boswick," Margo answered. "Remember Jack? His son, and promising to be just as awful as his father. All macho brawn and not a brain in his head. He's eighteen and quite the athlete—holds a lot of appeal for some of the younger boys. I don't know," she said with a sigh, rubbing a hand across her forehead. "It's not that Brad has really done anything. I know he drinks on occasion, but he is of age. I just don't like him and I worry about his influence on Steven. But Ken and I figure we have to trust Steven, let him develop his own judgment. He's not a little boy anymore. One more year of school and he'll be out in the real world." She sighed again. "We're hoping that if we don't interfere, he'll outgrow Brad before too much longer."

Anne's smile was reassuring. "Try not to worry about it so much. You've done a good job raising those boys. Steven's just at that awkward age, chafing against the restrictions of childhood and worried about taking on the adult responsibilities he sees looming not too far ahead. He'll come out of it okay. *We* all did, didn't we?"

"Yes, but—"

"But nothing. I'm sure we all drove our parents batty with doubts at about the same age. Think about it. Remember some of those parties you went to?" Anne grinned. "I heard about them."

Margo laughed. "You're right. They were pretty wild, weren't they? But," she added, "it would be nice if Steven were more like you were. Nice and quiet."

Anne grimaced. "I was *too* good. That's not right, either. But it was only because I was too scared and shy to get up to anything. And besides, the boys never did ask me out—I was taller than most of them."

"What was it they called you? 'Stork'?"

"You *would* remember," Anne groaned. "Whatever you do, Margo, don't remind the others. I don't want that started again."

"It's not too likely," Margo said with a laugh, looking her up and down. "You've come a long way since those days."

"Thank goodness. Now, what have we got to do to finish getting ready for this party of yours?"

CHAPTER TWO

THERE WAS A LULL in the party after Margo's delicious meal had been eaten. People sat clustered in little groups near the pool, chatting with the ease of long-time friendship, as the evening sun slanted long, golden rays across the yard, deepening the green of the surrounding trees and lawn.

Anne sat in a quiet corner, partially hidden by one of the planters full of bright-red geraniums decorating the cedar deck that stretched from the house to the pool. She leaned back against a rough stucco wall, sipping an icy drink. She knew all the people Ken and Margo had invited, some better than others. She hoped that, in time, some of those old friendships could be recaptured and grow, now that she was back.

Anne put down her glass and laced her fingers around her knees. The party, she knew, would soon get its second wind. Already the laughter was rising above a quiet murmur as drinks were finished and replenished. Soon there would be music, some dancing and the inevitable horseplay in the pool.

Anne found she almost always had to make a concentrated effort to join in the party mood. Quiet and contemplative by nature, she preferred meeting people on a one-to-one basis. Ken, she knew, was much the same. Not only had they both inherited their father's height and blondness, but they had his serious nature, as well. Their mother, Lillian, was the lively member of the family. Anne had to smile, thinking of how her mother liked to entertain. She wouldn't have been hiding behind a planter full of flowers. She'd be right in the middle of things, undoubtedly surrounded by a crowd of people laughing at her sharp wit and infallible sense of humor. She had an easy-going, forthright manner that Anne admired and had tried to emulate over the years.

It wasn't long before someone realized Anne wasn't with the crowd around the pool. Wayne Boychuck was a stocky man with a barrel chest and thinning hair who had married Anne's best friend, Judy, right after high school. The three of them had always been friends, it seemed, and had kept in close touch over the years. Wayne was standing by the pool, drink in hand, when he spotted Anne behind the planter.

"Hey, Stork!"

Anne grimaced. She should have known someone would bring up that despised nickname again. Trust it to be Wayne.

"Come on, Stork," he called, a grin splitting his round face. "Join the party!"

Anne stood, straightening her skirt. She glanced at a laughing Judy, smiled and winked, then sauntered toward Wayne, keeping her eyes directly on his face. His grin had turned into a somewhat self-conscious smile by the time she reached him and he took a hasty swallow from his glass.

Anne put her hands on his shoulders and looked demurely into his eyes. "You bellowed, Chuckie?"

Wayne took a step backward. "Ah, c'mon, Annie—not that!" He hated his high-school appellation as much as she did hers.

Anne widened her eyes and blinked at him. "But 'Chuckie' is so cute!" She leaned a little closer. "Just like you," she purred, and pushed hard against his shoulders. Wayne hit the water with a splash.

Anne stood with her hands on her hips, watching with a grin as Wayne sputtered to the side of the pool amid howls of laughter. "Oh, Chuckie," she said with mock consternation. "Did you slip?"

Wayne hauled himself onto the edge of the pool, wiping a hand across his dripping face, and joined in the laughter surrounding him. "I'm gonna get you for this, Annie," he warned.

"Big talker," Anne said with a toss of her head, and turned away, smiling widely.

There was a stranger watching her, inscrutable topaz eyes gleaming beneath an errant lock of russet hair.

Caught in her playful role, Anne reacted spontaneously. One hand on an out-thrust hip, she looked at him, her brows arching over eyes lit with genuine appreciation. "Well," she murmured, blatantly flirtatious, "and *who* are you?" She saw a spark flash, then fade in those remarkable eyes.

Laughing, Margo came to stand beside her. "Anne, meet Rob MacNeil, our new neighbor. Rob, this is Ken's sister, Anne."

He certainly matches Margo's description, Anne thought, her eyes lingering in spite of herself. She smiled politely, wishing she hadn't acted in such a provocative manner and hoping he wouldn't take it seriously.

She needn't have worried. There was a look of derision in the topaz eyes, a hint of contempt curling his well-cut lips.

"Anne," he said, acknowledging her with a curt nod before turning his attention to Margo. "Sorry I couldn't make it sooner," he added, his deep voice softening noticeably. "But I was having trouble with one of the mares."

"Ruby?" Ken asked, coming up behind. "She hasn't foaled already, has she?"

Rob shook his head. "I thought she might be starting, but Archie assured me she was just restless. Still, I didn't want to leave until I was certain."

"Did you eat?" Margo asked.

Rob turned back to her with a smile. "I grabbed something before I came over, thanks, Margo."

"How about some dessert," Margo persisted. "There are plenty of strawberries left."

"Maybe later. What I need right now is a swim."

"Go for it," Ken said. "I'll have a beer waiting for you when you come out."

Rob acknowledged his offer with a wave of his hand as he walked around the pool to the deep end.

Anne was not used to being ignored and there was no doubt in her mind that Rob had done just that. Piqued and puzzled by his cold reaction to her, she went to take a seat beside Wayne's wife, Judy. She smiled as she sat down, but her eyes were on Rob as he stripped off his shirt and flung it to one side before stepping onto the diving board.

She wasn't the only woman who watched. Most turned their eyes to him as he stood for a moment on the edge of the board.

He was a well-muscled man, with wide shoulders tapering to narrow hips covered by brief, navy-blue jogging shorts. His face was too craggy and lined to be conventionally handsome, but there was a dynamic air of masculinity about him that was very attractive. Anne watched through eyes narrowed with unwonted appreciation as he took a springing step, raised his arms over his head and knifed cleanly into the water.

Why couldn't he have been bandy-legged and balding, Anne thought with a hint of dismay. The man's presence would be impossible to ignore. Her initial reaction to his physical attributes cautioned her she should do just that.

"Mmm," Judy sighed as he emerged a few moments later, hair sleeked back over a wide forehead. "I love Wayne dearly, but there's nothing like the sight of a handsome man to set the old blood racing." She grinned at Anne, her gray eyes crinkling at the corners. "Rob MacNeil's presence has added a bit of spice to more than one marriage around here."

"Is that what happened to you?" Anne teased. She reached over and patted Judy's very pregnant stomach. "Congratulations, by the way. And Judy—I hope—well, I just hope everything is okay this time." Judy's first pregnancy had ended at seven months in a stillborn birth and this second one had been a long time in happening.

"According to the doctor, everything is fine," Judy said with calm assurance. "And I believe her. They've done every test there is and everything is normal." She winced suddenly and shifted in her chair. "And this baby keeps kicking like a football player! I will be glad when it's all over, though," she admitted. "Poor Wayne's a nervous wreck, fussing over me constantly..." She giggled suddenly. "'Chuckie'—I haven't heard him called that in years...and I think that dip in the pool relaxed him considerably, Anne."

Anne laughed. "And, knowing Wayne, he's so busy plotting revenge, he won't have time to worry about the baby."

"Good. He's been far too tense lately. He just won't be convinced everything is okay."

"Well, it won't be long now. What—about two weeks?"

"About. And it's nice you'll be here for the birth, Anne. I'm glad you're back, although I have to admit I'm kind of surprised."

Anne sat back in the lawn chair, straightening her skirt as she crossed her legs. "Most people are," she said. "But it feels right to me—for now, anyway. Who knows? Maybe I'll start feeling restless in a year or two and want to move on." She shrugged. "I'll see. Tell me, Ju—"

She stopped abruptly as Wayne, coming up from behind, picked her up, chair and all. Straining, he carried her toward the pool, egged on by cheers and laughter.

Anne clung tightly to the arms of the chair, hoping he wouldn't drop her. "Wayne—put me down!"

"Sure thing, Annie," he said, puffing. "You weigh a ton." He dumped her, chair and all, into the water.

Anne surfaced quickly, hiding a grin at the laughter that greeted her. Wading through the chest-deep water, she pulled herself out of the pool and stood a few feet from Wayne. Blinking water from her eyes, she stared at him in hurt accusation. "Why did you do that, Chuckie?" she asked, putting a little catch in her voice. She held up her hands and looked down at herself, then back to him. "I'm—I'm all *wet*!"

Anne was quite willing to continue playing her little game if it would make Wayne forget about his worries for a while and she wasn't averse to the laughter of the people around her. Pushing out her bottom lip in a pout, she plucked at her wet skirt and looked forlornly at Wayne, who gave himself a thumbs-up sign and mouthed, "Gotcha!"

It was then that she glanced past Wayne into eyes that glinted with unmistakable contempt. For her. Anne was confused. Why would a man who didn't know her, hadn't even spoken to her, feel that way? Unaccountably she felt hurt, as her eyes slid from Rob back to Wayne's laughing face. Unable to think of a witty response to Wayne, she wrinkled her nose at him and turned away.

Unfastening the knot in her skirt, she let it drop to the deck as she stepped to the edge of the pool and dove in.

She swam a slow length, then turned and started back again, puzzling over Rob MacNeil's attitude toward her. It was obvious he didn't like her, but why? There was no reason she could think of.

Telling herself she didn't care, she pulled herself out of the pool and picked up one of the towels Margo had left folded over the railing of the deck. As she dried off, she admitted to herself that maybe it was just as well he didn't seem to like her. If he had come on to her instead of turning away as he had... Anne's expression was somewhat rueful as she reached for the T-shirt she had put out earlier.

He was a very attractive man with an intense physical presence. She could have found herself knee-deep in a relationship she didn't want or need at this point in her life.

She pulled the T-shirt on over her head. It was bright green and oversize, reaching halfway down her thighs. Leaning her head to one side, she released her sodden hair from its braid and raked her fingers through it until it fanned across her shoulders; then, giving her head a little shake, she straightened.

"Having fun?" Margo asked. She had brought out a coffee urn and was busy setting it up on a picnic table near the patio doors off the kitchen.

Anne nodded, wiping the towel across her face one more time. "It's been great seeing everyone again," she said. "Is that coffee ready?"

"Yep, help yourself. You know," she added, lowering her voice, "you may have made a splash with Wayne—" she grinned "—but you made a hit with Rob."

Anne looked at her in total disbelief. "Wishful thinking, Ms Matchmaker. The man looked at me as though I'd just crawled out from under a rock. You're way off base on this one." She held a Styrofoam cup under the spigot on the urn and filled it with coffee.

"Don't be so sure, Anne," Margo said. "I thought the water might start boiling in the pool, the way he was watching you while you were swimming. In fact, he's hardly taken his eyes off you since he got here."

She was nodding with obvious satisfaction. "Yep, you've really made a hit, Annie."

There was a part of Anne that wanted Margo to be right, the same traitorous corner of her heart that had led her, eyes closed, into Graham's arms. But there was no substance, no soul to feelings like that. "You're wrong, Margo," Anne said, glad that she was. She had just cleared her life of one set of complications and didn't want more.

She stirred cream into her coffee and frowned, looking at Margo. "The man hasn't said two words to me—quite literally. I really think you're making something out of nothing. I wish you wouldn't. It makes me feel uncomfortable."

"But, Anne—"

"Please, Margo. It's going to be very embarrassing if he overhears any of this. And while Graham may not have been the love of my life, he did mean something to me. I need time to sort it all out, put it into perspective."

Margo sighed. "All right. I'll lay off the teasing."

Anne flashed her a smile. "Thanks. And one more thing—please convince that big brother of mine that I really don't need anyone looking in on me while you're gone. The boys and I will be just fine."

"That may be impossible," Margo said with a laugh. "But I'll give it my best shot."

Anne took her coffee and went over to the pool again. She sat back down in her lawn chair, catching snatches of conversation from around her, but her attention was on the deep rumble of Rob MacNeil's voice as he talked to Ken and some of the other men. She thought she could detect a faint, softening burr to his words, but when she tried to listen a little closer, someone turned up the music and a rock beat blared from the speakers Ken had set up outside the living room.

Wayne stood before her, hands up and fingers snapping to the music. "C'mon, Stork. Let's dance."

Anne shook her head and looked at him in mock exasperation. "Go dance with your wife, Wayne. Leave me alone."

"She won't dance with me," Wayne complained. "She says she's too pregnant." He held out a hand. "Come on."

"There's no one else dancing," Anne objected.

"Someone's got to be first."

"Does it always have to be you? All right, all right." She sighed and stood up. "But if you call me 'Stork' one more time, I'll have to take drastic action."

"Promises, promises," jeered Wayne. He led her to dance near the speakers where the music was loudest.

It was impossible not to have fun with Wayne. He hammed it up considerably, and his behavior was as outrageous as it had always been. Laughing, Anne matched him step for step, hardly faltering when she turned around to briefly meet contemptuous topaz eyes.

He's got the problem, not me, Anne thought, turning away with a toss of her head. He might be physically attractive, but his manner was boorish and rude, at least where she was concerned, and she'd had enough of those glowering, unprovoked looks. But while she told herself his dislike didn't bother her, some of her enjoyment of the party vanished.

IT WAS MUCH LATER when Anne walked Wayne and Judy to their car.

"I had fun tonight," Judy said. She smothered a yawn. "I should sleep like a log." She rubbed her stomach. "If junior settles down, that is."

Anne put a hand on Judy's stomach and felt a little foot kick under her palm. She laughed in delight. "That must be the most wonderful feeling!"

"It is," Judy agreed, smiling contentedly. "Just wait until it's your turn."

"That'll be a while yet," Anne said somewhat wistfully. "Wayne, make sure you let me know as soon as the baby's here."

"I'll be shouting it from the rooftops," Wayne said, opening the car door for Judy.

"A phone call will do. Don't forget."

"He won't," Judy promised. "You'll be one of the first to know. Good night, Anne. Call me soon."

"Will do. 'Night." She stood there for a moment after they drove away, glad her old friends were still happy together. "I just hope this baby is all right," she murmured to herself as she turned back toward the house.

It was a calm night. The day's heat had mellowed, and felt soft against her skin. She breathed deeply, unable to get enough of the heady, nighttime scents. She lingered in the garden under the deeper darkness of the trees, listening to the rustle of leaves stirred by a soft breeze.

BY THE TIME SHE RETURNED to the house, everyone but Rob MacNeil had gone. He sat on the deck, drinking coffee with Ken and Margo. Resisting the urge to slip quietly up to her room, Anne joined them.

Ken smiled at her lazily. "Enjoyed yourself, did you?"

Anne nodded. "It was great. Thanks, you two." She sat down beside Margo, avoiding a direct look at Rob. He sat across from Ken, his long bare legs stretched out before him as he cradled a mug of coffee in lean, square-tipped fingers. "It's funny," she added after a moment, "but I feel as if I've been away only a short time, as if I just picked up where I left off."

"I'm glad," Margo said. "I was—" She halted at the sound of a car turning into the driveway. "Steven's home."

The car stopped by the house and Steven got out. No sooner had he shut the car door than the driver peeled away with a spray of gravel and a blare of the horn. Anne winced as the raucous sounds shattered the still of the night.

"Who was that?" Rob asked with a dark frown.

"Brad Boswick," Ken answered, his lips tightening. "Jack's son. Do me a favor, Rob," he added. "Keep an eye on Steve while we're gone. If he shows even a sign of getting into trouble, put him to work on your place—hard work."

"Will do," Rob said.

Anne frowned indignantly at Ken. "I can handle Steven, Ken," she said, then turned to Rob, adding rather stiffly, "there's no need to concern yourself, Mr. MacNeil."

Thick dark brows rose above glinting eyes. "I promised your brother I'd keep an eye on things and

I'll do just that." There was the remnant of a Scottish burr in the quietly spoken words.

"My brother doesn't seem to realize I'm quite capable of looking after everything. All by myself," she added with emphasis.

"Annie," Ken said warningly.

"I'm sorry Ken, but either you trust me to care for your sons or you don't." The words sounded harsher than she had meant them to, but resentment was rising in her with every look from Rob. His eyes were stony and cold.

Anne stood up abruptly, flashing a brief smile of apology toward Ken and Margo. "I think I'll turn in now," she said, and left quickly.

She went directly to her room. Leaving the light off, she sat at the window, fidgeting as anger pinged through her.

It was a new feeling, this not being liked by someone, and it was made worse by the fact that her initial reaction to Rob had been one of attraction. What was his problem? Why didn't he like her? He seemed friendly enough toward everyone else, man or woman, from what she had seen, and Ken obviously held him in high regard. Anne sighed and rested her head against the cool pane of glass, welcoming a fresh wisp of breeze against her heated face.

This morning, coming home had seemed the perfect thing to do.

CHAPTER THREE

AS PEARL-GRAY LIGHT stole across the eastern sky, coyotes keened a last chorus from a distant hill. A whitethroat sparrow awoke to greet the new day with sleepy song.

Anne sat cross-legged on the sparse, wiry grass covering the sandy soil of a bluff overlooking the Assiniboine River. She watched as the golden rim widened and reached across the sky, gilding the scattering of thin, wispy clouds. The wide, green-brown river, deceptively lazy, curled beneath the high, sloping bluff. On the far, lower side of the river, wheat fields turned bright green under the rising sun.

For millenia, the river had been a highway to the interior of Canada. Indians had used it, as had the voyageurs seeking beaver pelts. Traders from Hudson Bay outposts had been at home on the river, and to European settlers eager to break fertile prairie soil, it had been the gateway to a new life.

In the absolute stillness of dawn, the river's surface was glassy smooth, a mirror for the red-winged blackbird flashing scarlet epaulets from an overhanging willow branch. Its clear, liquid song easily reached Anne, as did the soft, subtle perfume from the wild prairie roses blooming in pale pink profusion on the bank below her. Lifting her face to catch the sun's rays, she inhaled deeply, feeling last night's tension dissipate.

Anne was contemplative as she watched the river drift past. Her thoughts turned to Rob MacNeil. His attitude toward her rankled, as did the fact that she was unable to stop it from bothering her. And underneath it all was the rather uncomfortable knowledge that she had been easily attracted to the man.

Who wouldn't be? she wondered rather ruefully as again the picture of him standing poised on the end of the diving board flashed before her mind's eye. She sighed and dug at the sandy soil with her heel, annoyed that her quiet, orderly return home should suddenly feel compromised; annoyed, as well, that she felt attracted to a man who didn't even like her.

As she sat lost in thought, morning strengthened with the promise of heat to come. *It's time I got back,* she thought, standing. She stretched her long limbs and dusted off bits of pine needles clinging to her legs and started off. But at the last moment she took the path through the trees, knowing it would lead to Rob MacNeil's house. She wanted to see the home of the man who had been in her thoughts all morning.

She ran a bit, following the path as it cut down through a drop in the land before curving back along the crest of the high riverbank. Here, where the ground held more moisture, trembling aspen grew thick and the underbrush was high. The air felt cool and damp, rich with verdant odors.

A sudden scrambling in the brush startled Anne and she stopped, head tilted to one side as she listened. A rabbit darted out from a clump of buffalo berry and raced away. Seconds later, an Irish setter appeared in hot pursuit.

Anne put two fingers in her mouth and let out a piercing whistle. The dog skidded to a stop, then turned and looked at her, panting heavily. Unexpectedly it came toward her, tail wagging cautiously. Anne held out a hand and the dog swiped at it, dropping its hindquarters as its tail started wagging furiously.

"Who are you?" Anne murmured with a little laugh as she stroked the silky, deep red ears. "And why are you chasing little bunnies?"

With a final, sloppy lick, the dog ran back, nose to the ground, trying to recapture the rabbit's scent. Knowing the rabbit would be out of harm's way by now, Anne turned away, chuckling at the dog's frantic sniffing. Picking up her pace, she ran around the curve in the path and started up the slope.

She scarcely heard the staccato of hoofbeats before the horse was upon her. With a cry of surprise, she threw herself to one side as the horse, snorting in alarm, reared, almost unseating its rider. Pain stabbed through her ankle as she fell to the ground and a dark wave of dizziness muffled the rider's curse as he struggled to bring the horse under control. *It* would *be him,* Anne thought through the haze of pain.

Rob MacNeil slid off the horse and, with a gentle hand on its muzzle, calmed it with soothing words. He dropped the reins and squatted beside Anne. "Are you all right?" he demanded gruffly, the Scottish burr a little more pronounced than it had been the night before.

Anne pushed herself into a sitting position. "I'm fine," she mumbled, avoiding his eye.

"Are you sure?" he insisted. "You look kind of white."

Anne risked a glance at his face. She fully expected him to light into her, bawling her out for being on his land and scaring his horse. But there was nothing but concern in his eyes and in his voice.

"Um, my ankle," she said, wincing as she straightened her left leg. "It's—it's sprained, I think."

"Let me take a look." He ran his fingers over her ankle with a lightness that belied the strength in his lean, work-hardened hands. "It's already starting to swell," he said. "Here—"

He was interrupted by the horse coming up from behind and lowering its head until its muzzle was resting on his shoulder. Its ears were pricked and its round brown eyes bright with curiosity. "Back off, Cinnabar," he said with a laugh. "Let me get the lady on her feet." He turned back to Anne. "What about it? Can you get up?"

Anne nodded and scrambled up, careful not to put any weight on her ankle. Already it was throbbing painfully and she could feel the skin starting to tighten. There was no way it would take her weight. *Great,* she thought with dismay, *just great. I really need this.*

"I'm not going to be able to walk," she said rather stiffly as she sank back down to the ground.

"I didn't think so," Rob said. "It should be bound," he added.

Anne was frowning against the pain. "With what?"

He looked at her brief shorts and T-shirt. "Obviously not with anything you're wearing." He pulled his own well-worn T-shirt over his head. "This'll do."

He wrapped the bottom hem in his hands and with a twist of his wrists tore the shirt into halves and then into strips.

Kneeling on the ground in front of her, he lifted her leg with gentle hands and rested it across his thighs. Quickly he wrapped strips of cloth around the ankle and under her instep, tucking the loose ends in neatly. "That should keep it from jarring," he said, looking up. "All right?"

Anne nodded. The pain had subsided to a dull ache throbbing against the makeshift bandage. "Thanks."

"No problem." Rob stood up, extending his hand. "Here—you can ride Cinnabar back. It's all her fault, anyway." He closed his hand over Anne's and pulled her carefully to her feet. "Of course, you didn't help by squealing like a frightened rabbit and hurling yourself into the bush."

"It's pretty hard to hold your ground with several hundred pounds of horseflesh in your face," Anne retorted, steeling herself as she leaned against the whipcord strength of his bare arm and shoulder.

"What were you doing prowling around here, anyway?"

"I was out for a walk," she said, hopping painfully toward the horse.

"It's—"

"I know it's your property," she interrupted. "I'm sorry, but I haven't quite adjusted to the fact that it's no longer ours." Pain made her voice sound irritable and she felt his body stiffen.

"I was going to say that it's a beautiful morning for a walk," he said quietly. "And as far as the land goes, I'm sorry your family had to let it go, but I'm not going to make apologies for being able to buy it from them. Can you ride?'' he asked abruptly.

Wishing she could manage without his help, Anne clutched at his shoulder for support. ''Don't worry. I can. You won't have to carry me.''

''No chance,'' he snorted. ''You aren't exactly a featherweight, are you? Wait—let's see if she'll let you get on her right side. It'll make it easier for you.''

''What if she won't let me?'' Anne asked, hobbling to the other side of the mare.

''Then you'll end up with a few more scratches on that derriere of yours. Grab the mane now. Let her take your weight while I give you a boost.''

Because Rob had been riding bareback, there was no way Anne could get on the horse without considerable help. She was very conscious of the feel of his hands through the thin material of her shorts as he lifted her until she was able to throw her left leg over the horse's back. A stab of pain shot up her leg as her ankle hit the mare's belly, and a little moan escaped her lips.

''You okay?'' Rob asked, his eyes intent as he looked up at her, his steadying hand on Cinnabar's neck.

Anne nodded, biting her lip to stop the tears pricking her eyes.

To her relief, he picked up the reins and started walking, the mare falling into step behind him. It would have been intolerable if he had climbed up on the horse behind her. He had been polite enough and certainly gentle while he had bandaged her ankle, but Anne still sensed that he didn't like her much. To have him sitting behind her on the horse, their bodies touching and swaying to the plodding rhythm... Anne twisted her fingers in the horse's mane and frowned.

Except for the jingle of the bridle and the clop of Cinnabar's hooves, they made their way in silence. Rob walked at a steady pace, his stride loose and easy. He now wore nothing but jeans, bleached pale blue with age, and well-worn moccasins on his bare feet. Anne watched him over the mare's head, her eyes narrowing in appreciation. The sun glinted on his sleek russet hair and warmed the bronzed skin of his broad back. Already she knew that it felt like heated satin beneath her fingers.

She bit back a little moan of annoyance and gave her head a shake, irritated by the direction her thoughts were taking. She usually wasn't one to be caught in adolescent flights of fantasy. Bodies had sensation, not sense, and there was no way she would succumb to purely physical demands. *Not that he's likely to offer,* she thought wryly. He'd made it pretty obvious she wasn't his type.

Margo saw them through the kitchen window. She came out onto the back steps and waited while Rob led the horse to the house. She was wearing a cotton robe over her pajamas and her dark eyes still had a look of sleepiness.

"What happened?" she demanded as they stopped by the bottom step.

"She turned her ankle," Rob said before Anne could answer. "It looks bad. I think she should be taken in for X rays."

"It's not that bad," Anne protested, but without much conviction. Her ankle felt heavy and ached with dull throbbing pain.

"I'll go get Ken up," Margo said. "Make like a hero, Rob, and bring her into the house." The screen door shut behind her.

Anne looked down onto the top of Rob's head as he tied the reins to the porch railing, and wished it had been Ken who had come to the door. She would rather submit to her brother's help than Rob's. She grimaced a bit as he glanced up and caught her eye.

"Come down on the right side. You can land on your right foot that way."

Anne leaned forward on the horse's neck and slowly lifted her leg, resting it for a moment on the broad rump. Biting her lip against the pain, she slid off, feeling Rob's hands close around her waist.

"Looks like I'm going to have to carry you, after all," he said in a tone of resignation. "Unless you're up to hopping up those stairs on one foot."

Anne gritted her teeth and clung to his arm, knowing she wasn't. Trying would just make her look more foolish than she already felt.

He picked her up easily. As she felt the smooth, sun-heated skin of his bare chest and shoulders and smelled his warm masculine scent, Anne wished fervently that he hadn't used his T-shirt to wrap her ankle. The close, intimate touch was more than she wanted to feel with this man.

"The living room, I think," Rob said as he opened the door to the kitchen. "You should get that foot up. It's swelling fast."

By the time he had her in the living room, Ken had come in with Margo. He yawned and ran a hand through sleep-tousled hair. "What's she been up to?" he asked Rob.

"I was trying to avoid being made into hamburger," Anne answered, trying to lighten her mood as Rob sat her on the couch. She winced with pain as he straightened her leg and laid her foot gently on a cushion.

"What's that mean in English?" Ken asked as Rob moved away. Sitting down on the edge of the couch, he lifted her ankle to unwrap the makeshift bandage.

"She's scared of Cinnabar," Rob drawled. "She jumped into the bush when she saw us coming." He moved away and took a chair opposite the couch. "How bad is it?"

"I don't think anything is broken, but you're right. A doctor should look at it." He turned back to Anne and shook his head. "That's what you get for running around the country at the crack of dawn. Now maybe you'll learn to sleep in like normal people."

"I was all right until he came charging out of the bush on that horse of his." She scowled at the two men and then turned to Margo. "You wouldn't by any chance have coffee ready, would you?"

"Shouldn't we get her to the hospital first?" Margo asked Ken.

"You can't ask me to face that without a cup of coffee," Anne protested when she saw Ken was about to agree. "There's no need to hurry. I'm all right."

"But it must hurt," Margo objected. "It certainly looks painful."

Anne glanced down at her ankle. It was badly swollen and beginning to take on a dark hue. "It's not that bad now that it's not being banged around." She looked pleadingly at Margo. "I could really use a cup."

"All right," Margo said. "Rob?"

"Please," Rob said, leaning back in his chair, watching them through inscrutable eyes.

"I'll go up and finish getting dressed," Ken said, standing up.

Great, Anne thought as the two of them left the room, *leave me alone with him.* She glanced at Rob, who was watching her through half-closed eyes, his hands folded across his belt buckle and his long legs stretched out in front of him. She glanced away quickly and squirmed around on the couch until she was able to put her head down. That way she didn't have to look at him. Closing her eyes, she wished she had never thought of going for a walk that morning.

"Isn't it tomorrow that Ken and Margo leave on their trip?" he asked suddenly.

Anne nodded, her arm hiding her face from his gaze. Friends were driving them into Winnipeg in the early morning. From there they would take a plane to England. She didn't say anything, hoping Rob wouldn't bother to try to carry on a conversation with her.

Ken came back after a few minutes of uncomfortable silence, carrying an ice pack.

"Let's put this on that ankle, Annie. Maybe it'll keep some of the swelling down." He placed it carefully under her foot. "There. That'll hold it until you down that coffee and we get you to the hospital."

"You know, Ken," Anne began, "I'm not so sure I really need to go to the hospital. Just bandage it up good and tight and it'll be okay in a day or two."

"No way," Ken said firmly. "D'you think we're going to leave tomorrow not knowing if there's something more seriously wrong with that foot than a sprain? As it is—"

"You're not thinking of canceling, are you?" Anne interjected quickly, horrified at the thought.

Ken gave his head a shake. "After all that planning? No way. You might be immobile for a couple of days, but it's not like the boys need a lot of looking after. Besides, Rob will be around to lend a hand when you need it."

"I've already troubled Mr. MacNeil enough," Anne said hurriedly. "If I need anything, I'm sure Wayne will be only too glad to help."

Rob sat up straight in his chair, a dark line cutting his brow. "Don't you think Boychuck has enough on his mind right now without having to run after you? Leave him alone." He stood up abruptly. "Ken, tell the boys to call me if there's anything they need while you're gone." He went to the doorway, where he stopped and turned around. Ignoring Anne, he smiled at Ken. "I'll be off now. Have a good trip, and don't worry about things at this end. I'll see that everything is okay." He lifted a hand in salute and was gone.

Anne pushed herself up, scowling angrily. "How can you stand that man, Ken? He's so rude and—and arrogant!"

"He's okay," Ken said mildly, looking at his sister, his eyebrows raised in surprise. "You know, I was kind of hoping you two would hit it off."

"I'd like to hit *him*," Anne murmured in exasperation. "Really, Ken—I meant it when I said I don't want him interfering. He may be your friend, but he certainly isn't mine. I can manage just fine on my own."

"Oh, yeah? From the looks of that ankle you won't be up to much for the next week at least. Who's going to run into town for milk, or drive the boys to their baseball games . . . things like that?"

"It's my left ankle," Anne said. "I can still drive."

"Last time I looked, both cars were standard. You'll have a hell of a time working the clutch."

"Damn," Anne muttered, already chafing at the feeling of helplessness. "Still, if I have to ask anyone for help, I'd rather it was someone I knew—like Wayne."

"Rob was right about that, Anne. Wayne does have enough on his plate at the moment." Ken frowned at his sister, the lines cutting deep between his blue eyes. "What have you got against Rob, anyway?"

Anne scowled and pushed her hair back from her face. "I just don't like his attitude toward me."

"You sound like a twelve-year-old, Annie," Ken said disapprovingly. "Rob's a good man—a good neighbor. And my friend. Lighten up on the guy, will you? Give him a chance."

"In case you haven't noticed, big brother, the feeling seems to be mutual. Rob MacNeil doesn't like me any more than I like him, whatever the reason."

Margo came in, carrying the coffee. "Here you go, Annie," she said. "Drink it down, then we'll get you to the hospital. Where was Rob off to in such a hurry?" she asked Ken as she handed him his coffee. "He looked kind of angry."

Ken took his mug with a smile of thanks. "He and Annie were butting heads."

Margo sighed and sat down in the chair Rob had vacated. "Looks like our matchmaking plans are down the tubes.'' She took a sip of coffee. ''I'll have to warn your mom when we see her in England.''

Anne frowned at her sister-in-law. ''You mean you and my dear mother were planning on pairing me off with—with *him*?'' The tension and exasperation of the morning made her voice rise with indignation.

Margo grinned. ''Of course we were. Do you really think we could let a good-looking—single—man pass by without giving it a shot? Too bad you won't cooperate, Annie. We'd decided he'd be perfect for you.'' She appeared thoughtful as she took another sip of coffee. ''Still, there does seem to be some sort of reaction between the two of you. Maybe . . .''

Anne shook her head vehemently. ''Please, Margo, I'm not in the mood for this.'' She put her mug down on the coffee table. ''What I really want is to get this darned ankle checked, swallow a painkiller and try for a shower.'' She wrinkled her nose as she looked down on herself. ''I smell like a horse.''

''Right,'' Ken said, standing up. ''Let's get going then. Coming, Margo?''

Margo shook her head. ''I want to finish packing. And I think I'll whip up a batch of pancakes. It's the last breakfast I'll be making in a while. Might as well make it a good one.''

''Okay. We shouldn't be long, anyway. I can't see that they'll be that busy at this time of the day. Don't let Steve eat all those pancakes.'' He gave a helping hand to Anne. ''Come on, Annie. Let's get this over with.''

CHAPTER FOUR

ANNE AND THE BOYS settled quickly into a routine once Ken and Margo had left on their trip. Scott and Steven seemed happy to be with their aunt and were eager to help out. With her ankle tightly bound, Anne managed to swing around the house on a pair of crutches. She felt awkward but not totally incapacitated.

To Anne's relief, Rob MacNeil did not come around. He phoned each day, but waited until the boys were home from school and talked to them, not Anne. So far there had been no need to ask him for anything.

Anne hobbled out onto the deck one afternoon to sit beside the pool with a book and her reading glasses. She had discarded the crutches the day before and managed a cautious, limping walk. She was confident that within a couple of days her ankle would be back to normal, if somewhat weak.

She read beside the pool awhile. The day had a quiet, dreamy air about it and she enjoyed the peace. When she became hot, she unwrapped the bandage from her ankle and limped to the edge of the pool.

She wore a one-piece electric-blue bathing suit that fitted her curves like a second skin. The color lit her eyes until they seemed as blue as the sky overhead.

Sitting on the cement edge of the pool, she slowly lowered herself into the water, welcoming its silky coolness on her sun-heated skin. With a sigh of pleasure, she pushed away from the side.

Floating on her back, she stared dreamily into the sky, appreciating the contrast of the notched leaves spreading against the deep blue. She felt good, relaxed and at peace.

There was a sudden splash opposite her. A wave of water slapped across her face and filled her mouth. With a choking sputter, she stood up, coughing. *What—?*

The Irish setter she had last seen hot on the trail of a rabbit was swimming toward her, head held high. Anne could have sworn there was a grin on its face.

She wiped a hand across her face and grinned back. "You silly dog. Where did you come from?"

"He's mine, I'm afraid."

With a jerk of her head, Anne turned around. Rob MacNeil stood by the pool, a somewhat apologetic look on his face.

"I'm sorry about that," he said. "Blue—well, he's kind of exuberant. And he loves to swim."

"He does, doesn't he?" Anne had to laugh at the dog paddling madly around her.

"He's not supposed to be in the pool, but he got away on me. And he doesn't listen very well."

Anne looked at Rob in surprise. She would have expected a dog of his to be absolutely obedient.

"I came for a swim," Rob explained. "I didn't know you'd be using the pool. I'll come back some other time."

"Please don't leave on my account. I was just about to come out, anyway." Anne moved toward the steps. "Please—go ahead."

"Are you sure you don't mind?"

Was that a note of hesitation she heard in his voice? "Of course not. Ken told me you'd be using the pool. He didn't mention anything about the dog, though," she added with a grin as the animal swam to the steps and left the water to stand beside his master, where he gave his fur a furious shake.

Anne laughed. "Go for it—you're already soaked, anyway."

Rob grinned suddenly and joined her laughter with a rich chuckle. The dog waggled his rear end ecstatically and leaped around like a puppy.

"Blue," Rob commanded. "You stay now. Sit."

The dog sat—eventually. Anne was delighted and grinned widely. "You're right. He doesn't listen very well, does he?"

Rob shrugged. "He's a good dog. Just a little hyper."

"Is he a pup?"

"Actually," Rob said ruefully, "he's six years old. I kept thinking he'd settle down as he got older, but..." He squatted by the dog and rubbed the wet, deep red ears. "How's the ankle?" he asked.

Anne sat on the edge of the pool, feeling somewhat self-conscious in her bathing suit, glad Rob kept his gleaming topaz eyes on the dog and not on her. "It's almost back to normal," she said. "A little weak, but it should be all right in a few days."

"Good. And how are things around here?"

"No problems—the boys take care of everything. They're really very good kids."

"No problems with Steve?"

"Nothing I can't handle," Anne replied with a touch of asperity. Things might have started out on a friendlier note than usual, but she still didn't want him interfering.

"Listen—"

"Aren't you going for that swim?" Anne interrupted. She slid into the pool again and swam quickly to the far side. When she turned around to swim back, she saw that Rob had pulled off his T-shirt and was walking toward the diving board.

Returning to the shallow end, Anne pulled herself out of the pool and watched him. She had nothing but appreciation for the way he looked, the way he moved. And this time she knew exactly how that bronzed skin felt under her fingers, had knowledge of the strength in his broad shoulders.

Leaning her head to one side, she wrung water from her hair, an expression of dismay flitting across her face. How could she react this way to a man she scarcely knew, a man she wasn't even sure she liked?

In spite of herself, her eyes returned to him as he stood poised on the edge of the diving board before plunging into the water.

As Anne watched Rob swim, she wondered again at the negative attitude he so obviously had toward her. It made it hard for her to see him objectively. Ken seemed to think a lot of him, as did Margo and the boys. What did she herself think of him?

Thoughts of his physical presence rushed to mind, but she pushed those aside impatiently. That he was physically attractive to her was patently obvious.

He seemed to be stern and somewhat arrogant, a distant man. Even when he talked to Ken or the others there was an air of remoteness about him, and she wondered briefly what caused it. But she'd caught glimpses of a sense of humor she knew she could appreciate, and there had been a definite air of gentleness about him when he'd taken care of her ankle.

As she sat thinking, Blue came up to her, tail wagging happily. With a smile Anne rubbed the damp patch of fur between his ears.

"No licking," she admonished as the dog tried to swipe her face with his tongue. "I don't like doggy drool!" The dog stretched out his head, eyes half-closed in bliss as she scratched behind his ear.

Anne turned her eyes back to the pool, watching Rob's sleek head cut through the water. The dog, sensing her attention drifting from him, whined deep in his throat and laid a paw on her wrist, insisting on more scratches. Laughing, Anne rubbed between his ears.

"Let's face it," she murmured. "Anyone who owns a goofy dog like you can't be all bad!" She pushed gently on the side of his head. "Go lie down now."

To Anne's surprise, the dog flopped down beside her, muzzle resting on his forepaws as he gazed up at her, his eyes soulful and adoring.

Obviously she'd made a hit with Blue, if not with his master. Leaning back, she swung her legs in the water and frowned, irritated with herself for not being able to put the whole thing out of her mind. But she couldn't help it. Like it or not, Rob's attitude bothered her and she wished she knew what lay behind his obvious disapproval.

She sat up straight as Rob climbed out of the pool, deciding she wasn't going to let his attitude cloud hers. She would be polite and try to be friendly. Maybe it would have some effect on him. Smiling a shade cautiously, she stood up and walked toward him, averting her eyes as he rubbed a towel across his gleaming torso.

"There's nothing like a swim on a hot day, is there?" she asked lightly. "Can I get you something to drink? There are soft drinks in the fridge, or lemonade if you'd rather."

There was surprise in the way his eyebrows arched over his eyes, but no spark of warmth answered her tentative offering. "No, thanks," he said briefly. "I've got to get going. Thanks for the use of the pool."

He snapped his fingers and the dog bounded to its feet, bumping into Anne. She buckled her leg instinctively to prevent her weight from being thrown onto her weak ankle, but before she could fall, Rob's hand shot out and grabbed her arm.

Anne clutched at him, steadying herself. "That was close," she murmured, her lashes dropping to her cheeks. He was close. Too close. She could smell his damp skin, feel it where her fingers curled over his arm. Instead of pushing herself away, she looked up at him.

He was gazing at her through narrowed eyes, eyes that flashed briefly as his nostrils flared and his firm lips parted. For an instant it looked as though those lips would descend to claim hers...and then he moved away.

"Thanks again for the swim," he said impersonally as he picked up his T-shirt. "Let's go, Blue." The dog ran ahead of him down the steps leading from the deck to the lawn. With a polite nod toward Anne, Rob followed.

"Goodbye to you, too," Anne said under her breath to his broad, retreating back. She limped to a deck chair and sat down, shaking her head in disbelief. How could she have reacted like that? She couldn't deny that for a brief moment she had wanted him to kiss her, to feel his stern lips soften as they touched hers....

Anne gave a little groan and shook her head again. How could she feel such an attraction to a man she scarcely knew, a man who seemed to feel nothing but disdain for her?

And *why* did he feel as he did? People almost always liked her, enjoying her sense of humor and her easygoing, straightforward manner. Why didn't Rob?

She brooded about it for a few moments, then shrugged it off. If he didn't like her, that was his problem, not hers. She picked up the book she had brought out with her and pushed on dark-rimmed glasses.

She might have stopped brooding over why he didn't seem to like her, but she didn't stop thinking about him. As she leaned back in the chair, trying to read, he kept slipping into her thoughts. She could see the sun glinting on his russet hair, on his strong arms as he easily swam the length of the pool. And his eyes... The book dropped from her hands and lay unnoticed on the ground beside her chair.

There was more to those eyes than their unusual color, she thought suddenly. Had there been a shading of pain or sorrow in them, or was it just her imagination? She sighed again and picked up her book, determined to read. What did it matter?

ANNE PUT DOWN the report cards she had been examining and beamed at the two boys. "Good grades, guys. Your parents will be pleased."

"When will they phone?" Scott asked. He was lolling beside the pool, noisily sucking a soft drink through a straw.

"Probably not until the weekend," Anne told him. "They're leaving for France sometime tomorrow and they said they'd phone when they got settled. Scott, could you please drink that more quietly?"

Scott looked up at her and grinned. "Sorry."

"Pig," Steven muttered.

Anne held up her hand as Scott opened his mouth to retaliate. "Stop it right there," she demanded mildly. "No name-calling allowed when I'm around. Now I think we should celebrate tonight. It's the last day of school and you both passed. Let's go out for hamburgers before the baseball game."

"They're gonna have hot dogs at the game, Annie," Scott informed her.

Anne made a face. "Boiled wieners on soggy buns. Wouldn't you rather have a thick, juicy cheeseburger with fries and a milk shake at Bud's?"

"I sure would," Steven said.

"Me, too," Scott grinned.

"Then that's what we'll do. Let's get ready now. The game starts in a couple of hours."

"Are you going to play on the parents' team, Annie?" Scott asked.

"I'd like to," Anne answered. It had been a long time since she'd played a game of baseball, but she had always enjoyed it. "But my ankle isn't strong enough yet. I don't want to take a chance on turning it again." She stood up and started toward the house. "I'm going to change now," she told the boys over her shoulder. "You guys get ready, too. Just wear whatever you would to the ball game."

It wasn't until they were in the car that Anne realized her ankle was still too tender to engage the clutch without it causing her pain.

"Sorry, guys," she said. "I guess we'll have to call someone to come and pick us up. We'll get the hamburgers another night."

"I can drive, Annie," Steven said. "I got my beginner's."

"But can you drive a standard?"

Steven shrugged. "Yeah, no sweat."

Scott groaned from the back seat. "Oh, no—death!"

"Okay, Steve," Anne interjected quickly. "We'll give it a try." She knew Steven had been taking driver's education at school and probably would have had his license by now if Ken and Margo hadn't made him wait until they got back from their trip. "Just take it slow, okay?"

"*Very* slow," Scott said. "I'm too young to die!"

"Wanna bet?" Steven muttered as he opened his door and got out to come around to the driver's side.

"Keep it quiet, Scott," Anne warned as she slid across the seat. "I wouldn't let him drive if I didn't think he could do it."

After a jerking start, they were off. Anne felt uncomfortable at first, but soon realized that Steven was quite competent behind the wheel. She relaxed, but kept a watchful eye on the speedometer.

They spent an enjoyable hour over the meal and then left for the game, which was held down by the Assiniboine River. There were two back-to-back diamonds on spreading, lawnlike fields. Gnarled cottonwood, elm and oak trees spread shade along the riverbank.

As Steven and Scott left to find their friends, Anne spread out a blanket under one of the trees and sat down. She carefully arranged her skirt over her legs, then leaned back against the rough bark, looking around. She would have liked to play a game or two. None of the games played today would be taken seriously. It was a community event planned for young and old, and was strictly for fun.

Anne spotted Wayne and waved to him, hoping to see Judy, as well. "Hi," she said as he came over. "Where's your wife?"

"She didn't want to come," Wayne answered, flopping down beside her on the blanket. "She says she just wants a quiet, peaceful evening without me hovering over her. She said she'd call her mother if anything happened." He ran a hand through his thinning hair and sighed. "It's any day now, the doctor says. I'll sure be glad when it's all over."

Anne patted his arm sympathetically. "Don't worry so much, Wayne. It'll be okay. Just think. A month from now, you'll be complaining because you can't get a decent night's sleep for the baby crying."

"I sure hope so," Wayne said fervently.

"I know so. What d'you want, a boy or girl?"

"I don't care much just now, but—" he grinned "—I'm kinda partial to little girls. Must have something to do with having five younger brothers."

Anne laughed and nodded, remembering Wayne's large, boisterous family of boys. "A girl would be nice," she agreed.

"Are you playing, Anne?" Wayne asked. "We could use another woman on our team to keep things even."

Anne shook her head regretfully. "Can't—my ankle is still on the weak side and there's no way I'm going to risk turning it again."

"Tell you what. You do the hitting and I'll run for you."

"I'm not so sure I can hit. It's been years. But—okay, let's go for it." It would be a lot more fun than sitting around and watching.

"All right, then. I'll go let the others know."

After Wayne left, Anne saw that the boys' teams were getting ready to play, and moved her blanket closer to the diamonds to be in a good position to cheer for Scott.

She saw Rob as he stepped up to the group of boys clustered by the backstop. He was tossing a ball into the air and catching it with lazy ease. The boys gathered around him eagerly, laughing as he joked with them. Anne hadn't realized he'd become so involved with the community that he was coaching a baseball team. She watched thoughtfully as he treated the boys with a warmth and humor that was so different from the remote, unfriendly attitude he had toward her.

The game was fast and fun. Anne felt quite comfortable sitting in the dappled shade of an elm tree. When Wayne came over and offered her a canned drink, she took it with a smile of thanks.

"I wasn't sure if you drank beer," Wayne said, dropping down beside her. "But I figured I could always get you one later if you wanted." He took a long swallow from his bottle.

"This is fine, thanks, Wayne."

"S'okay." Wayne took another swallow. "All set to swat that ball into the river?"

Anne grinned and flexed her muscles. "You bet. Just let me at it."

"It's a little like old times, isn't it?" Wayne asked. He lay on his back with his hands behind his head, staring up into the tree. "Except Judy isn't here...and the next time she is, there'll be the baby." He let out a huge sigh. "With any luck," he muttered under his breath.

"Oh, Wayne—stop worrying!" Anne admonished gently. "Sit up and watch the kids play and think about how good yours is going to be in a few years." She gave him a playful jab in the ribs.

Wayne groaned and hit at her hand as he sat up. "Jeez, you're bossy," he grumbled. "It's about time you got married. You need a man to keep you in line."

"Keep your male chauvinism in the closet, Chuckie," Anne said. "I don't need a man for anything."

Wayne waggled his eyebrows suggestively. "Nothing?" he jeered.

Anne glared at him. "Don't be rude, Wayne. Be quiet and watch the game."

Wayne turned to watch. "He's pretty good with those kids," he said, gesturing toward Rob. "I was a bit surprised when he offered to coach. Even the guys with kids on the team don't want to be bothered."

"The kids do seem to like him." Anne took a sip of her drink. "What about you, Wayne? What d'you think of him?"

"He's all right. Can't say I really know him, though. He comes out for baseball, but doesn't go for a drink after the way the rest of the guys do. He kind of keeps to himself."

He was quiet for a moment and then turned to her with a wicked grin. "Why don't you go after him, Annie? He's rich enough from what I hear—and not bad looking for someone who's got all his hair."

Anne scowled at him. "Stop it, Wayne."

Wayne ignored her. "I think it's a good idea. And I'm sure Judy and Margo would agree. I'll bet they've already discussed it. C'mon Annie, go strut your stuff. You might just get yourself a man." He gave a howl of laughter and rolled away as Anne threatened him with her fist.

"If you can't behave yourself, Boychuck, then go sit somewhere else. I came here to cheer for Scott's team, not to listen to your drivel." She turned her back on him and glanced over to where Rob was standing. He was watching them, his dark frown evident even at a distance.

"Look," she said to Wayne. "He's glaring at us. Either he knows you're busy making plans to marry him off, or he thinks we should shut up and cheer for his team.''

''Are they winning?''

''I don't know. I think so, although they seem to drop the ball a lot.''

''So does the other team.'' Wayne finished the beer left in his bottle. ''I'm for another drink. What about you?''

Anne shook her head. ''No, thanks. And shouldn't you take it easy? Judy might need you tonight.''

To her surprise, Wayne didn't argue. ''You're right,'' he said as he stood up. ''I'll switch to pop.'' He grimaced. ''Even if it kills me. Hey, we're up after those kids. You ready?''

''As ready as I'll ever be,'' she answered, and then asked as he started to walk away, ''is—Rob on our team?''

''Best hitter we've got. Next to me, that is.''

Anne rolled her eyes and shook her head. ''Go away, Wayne.''

''I'm gone,'' he said cheerfully. ''But you'd better be nice to me or I won't run for you—providing you ever hit the ball, that is.'' He left, his usual grin splitting his round face.

Scott came running over to Anne as soon as the game was over. ''How'd I do?'' he asked, flopping down on the grass beside the blanket.

''Great,'' Anne said, smiling at his need for approval. ''You're a pretty good ball player.''

Scott grinned self-consciously. ''I'm better at hockey. But baseball's fun, too.''

''How do you like your coach?''

"He's great!" Scott said enthusiastically. "All the guys think so. He doesn't get mad if we don't do so good. The coach we had last year—Mr. Boswick—well, he was kinda mean sometimes." He sat up and waved to another boy. "Hey, Kris—c'mere!"

Obligingly the other boy trotted toward them.

"This is Kris," Scott said.

Anne smiled. "Hi, Kris."

"Hi," Kris answered shyly. He was a good-looking boy with dark blond hair and deep blue eyes. "Hey, Scott, Mom says it's all right if you spend the night, but make sure you ask your aunt first."

"Can I, Annie?" Scott asked. "We're making a tree house out behind his house. It's real neat."

"Your parents are Phil and Joan Wilson?" Anne wanted to make sure she had the right family.

"Yeah," Kris said with a nod.

"I'll talk to Mrs. Wilson," she told Scott. "But I don't see why you can't stay, if it's all right with her."

"It is," Kris said with assurance. "She likes it when Scott stays over, 'cause then I don't bug her for something to do all the time."

Anne laughed and reached for her purse. "Why don't you two run and get yourselves a drink?" She handed Scott some money. "Then you can come and watch me hit a home run or two."

Scott took the money. "Thanks, Annie. C'mon, Kris. There's enough for a hot dog too."

Anne made a face, wondering how Scott could possibly be hungry after the big supper he had consumed at the restaurant only a short while ago. She got up and brushed off her skirt, then went to find Kris's mother, a woman she remembered slightly from school. Joan Wilson assured her that Scott was no bother at all and would be dropped off at home sometime the next afternoon.

By the time Anne returned to where she had been sitting, Wayne was back to drag her off to the diamond for the game.

It was played strictly for laughs. In fact, Anne soon found out that the more laughs the better. Nobody really cared who won or lost; it was all done for fun. Even Rob hammed it up when it was his turn at bat. Still, when he hit the ball, it flew far into left field, and he jogged easily around the bases, bringing home two other players.

"You're up next," Wayne said, handing Anne a bat.

Anne took it and swung it experimentally. "Hope you've got your running shoes on. I intend to wallop that ball."

Rob frowned at her as she stepped up to home plate. "You don't plan on running, I hope. I doubt that ankle is strong enough yet."

"It isn't," Anne said, tapping the base with the tip of the bat. "Wayne's going to run for me."

"If she hits it," Wayne said, standing by the catcher.

"I'll hit it," Anne said confidently. "You'd better be ready."

Wayne grinned and winked. "I'm ready when you are," he said with a hint of a leer. Anne ignored him, but caught Rob's frown as he turned abruptly away.

The other team greeted Anne with catcalls and whistles as she stepped up to bat, the breeze swirling her skirt around her knees. Ignoring them, she grasped the bat and leaned to one side, waiting for the third ball to cross the plate before she swung. The bat connected with a jarring crack and sent the ball flying past the pitcher.

"Way to go, Annie!" Wayne shouted as he sprinted toward first.

To Anne's surprise and delight, the second baseman missed the ball and it bounced past the fielder. His short legs pumping, Wayne raced around the bases and slid home just ahead of the ball.

"Great legwork, Boychuck," Anne said with a grin as he picked himself up and dusted off his jeans.

"Couldn't have done it without you, Annie," he responded with mock modesty.

"Darned right," Anne retorted. She turned to hand the bat to the next player and caught Rob's look. It was nothing if not shot with distaste and dislike. Anne scowled back, angered that he should treat her with such coldness when he was so friendly toward everyone else. She had done nothing to warrant such behavior on his part. With a proud toss of her head, she walked away.

The sun was sinking low in the western sky by the time the games were finished. Anne saw Scott off with the Wilsons and looked around for Steven, anxious, by this time, to get home. He was nowhere to be seen.

Frowning, Anne approached Wayne as he was about to get into his car. "Have you seen Steven?" she asked. "He drove my car here—I can't manage the clutch yet."

Wayne shook his head. "I haven't seen him since his game earlier. He must have gone, Anne—nearly everyone else has. Listen, leave your car here. I'll drive you home and we can arrange to pick it up tomorrow."

Anne shook her head. "I should wait. He might have just gone for a ride with the other boys."

"If that's the case, he can get a ride home with them. I don't think you should have to hang around waiting for him. C'mon, get in."

Anne took one last look around the park, but even in the fading light, it was obvious Steven was not there. "All right," she said reluctantly. Opening the car door, she slid in, feeling worry mingled with her anger.

"Don't fret about him, Anne," Wayne said as they drove away. "He probably just lost track of time or something. He'll get home just after you do, looking all sheepish and apologetic. You know kids."

"I suppose so," Anne said with a sigh. "Listen, drop me off at the highway. I know you're in a hurry to get back to Judy."

"It's only a couple of minutes to the house. It's no problem."

"I know, but I wouldn't mind a bit of a walk. For all the balls I hit today, I didn't get a lot of exercise."

"If you insist..." They drove in silence for a few minutes. "So, what are you going to do to the kid when he gets home?"

"Find out what happened and talk about it," Anne said, "and then chain him in the basement until his parents get home."

Wayne laughed as he pulled the car over to the edge of the road and came to a stop. "Give it to him good, Annie. See you."

Anne got out of the car. "Thanks for everything. Tell Judy she missed a fun day. Bye, now." She waved as Wayne pulled back onto the highway, then stood watching the taillights disappear around a curve in the road, before she set off along the driveway leading to the house.

It was a soft, calm summer evening. The sun had slipped below the horizon, leaving a brilliant display of colored clouds to light the sky. As Anne walked, she startled a killdeer into flight, and its shrill cry echoed in the dusk.

Anne heard the music before she could see the house. Frowning, she quickened her step, still careful of her ankle. As she passed a grove of poplar trees, she could see the house, brightly lit. Steven had obviously come home.

There was a four-wheel-drive truck parked by the house. Anne took a quick look inside and saw that the keys were still in the ignition. At that moment someone emitted a string of expletives that was followed by a burst of raucous laughter and a splash from the pool. Impulsively Anne reached into the truck, took the keys and pocketed them.

Anne entered the living room, where rock music was blaring from the stereo, and peered outside through the patio doors. Steven and four other boys were lounging around the pool. As she watched, one of them, wearing only his briefs, took a long swallow from a bottle of beer and then staggered over to the diving board, clowning it up to the laughter of the other boys.

Anne's lips were tight as she switched off the stereo. She stood where she was, arms folded and one foot tapping in anger. She heard howls of protest from the boys, then Steven appeared at the doorway.

"I'll fix it," he called over his shoulder. As he turned around he saw his aunt and stopped in his tracks. "Oh—uh, hi, Annie." He made a feeble attempt to grin.

"Go out and tell the others the party is over, Steven."

Steven turned abruptly on his heel and went back outside. Anne could hear the murmur of voices and the clink of beer bottles being quickly put back into the case. She went outside.

Four boys regarded her warily. The other one stood beside the pool, a leer on his face as he picked up his jeans and started to pull them on over his wet briefs.

"Who drove?" Anne asked.

"Uh, Brad did," Steven answered.

Brad was obviously the one by the pool. It was just as obvious that he had been drinking considerably.

"Well, boys, I suggest you phone home for a ride. Brad's in no shape to drive."

Brad's chin jutted out aggressively and he glared at her. "Says who?"

"I do," Anne said calmly. "You've been drinking, Brad. You can't drive."

"I can handle it."

"Not behind the wheel of a car, you can't."

Brad's lips curled in a sneer and he insolently pulled up the zipper of his jeans. "Who's gonna stop me?"

Anne held up the keys she had taken from the truck. "I am."

Brad's face grew dark with anger. "Hey—you got no right to go taking my keys." He took a threatening step toward her. "Give 'em here."

Anne stood firm. "No, Brad, I won't. Quite frankly, at this point I'm having a hard time feeling concern for you, but I do care that you might injure—or kill—someone else if you drive in the condition you're in." She straightened her shoulders and thrust out her chin as Brad took another step.

Steven came quickly to stand beside her. "She's right, Brad. Leave it for tonight, eh? You can get the truck in the morning."

"I'm driving tonight," Brad said belligerently, raising a clenched fist. "You'd better gimme those keys or I'll—"

A deep voice spoke from behind Anne. "Or you'll what, Brad?"

Anne swung around. Rob stood just behind her and she felt a rush of relief.

Brad's aggressive stance disappeared like air from a popped balloon. Like all bullies, he would never stand up to someone stronger than himself. "Nothin'..." he mumbled, and turned away.

"All right, guys," Rob said. "My car's out in the driveway. Get your stuff together and get in. I'm driving you all home. That goes for you, too, Brad."

The boys, including Brad, moved quickly. Steven stood beside Anne, looking shamefacedly at his feet.

"I'm sorry, Annie," he mumbled.

Anne touched his arm briefly. He looked so young and contrite. "We'll—"

"I'll be back in twenty minutes," Rob cut in with an angry look at Steven. "You be waiting here."

Anne glared at him. "I can take it from here, thank you, Mr. MacNeil."

He turned to her, his eyes sweeping over her with a cold look. "Can you? Your brother told me to step in if things got out of hand. And they sure as hell have. I'll talk to Steve when I get back." He turned and walked away.

Anne frowned at his retreating back, then turned to Steven, who had the grace to appear apologetic.

"I'm really sorry, Annie. I didn't mean for this to happen."

"Steven, sit down." Anne sat on a lawn chair and gestured to the one across from her. She looked silently at him for a moment.

"You left me stranded tonight, Steven. How did you expect me to get home? You knew I couldn't manage the clutch."

"I was gonna come back. We just forgot about the time."

"You sneaked off from the game to come and party because you knew there would be no one here. And you were drinking. Don't bother to deny it—I can smell it on you." She sat back in the chair and folded her arms across her chest. "Not only is that expressly against your parents' wishes, it is illegal." She shook her head in disappointment. "I'm not impressed by what I saw here tonight, Steven. And as far as Brad goes..."

"He's a jerk," Steven said unexpectedly. "I never would have let him take those keys from you, Annie," he added earnestly.

Anne felt herself soften. "I know. Are you going to remain friends with him?"

Steven shrugged. "I dunno. We used to have lots of fun. But lately...all he wants to do is pick up some beer and go drinking somewhere. It's getting kinda boring. I got better things to do with my time."

"That's for sure." She studied him, her lips pursed thoughtfully.

He looked down, rubbing his knuckles in the palm of his hand. "I wasn't drinking to get drunk, Annie, not like the other guys. I just had a beer."

"You shouldn't have had even that."

"Yeah, I know." He looked up, his blue eyes, so like Ken's, troubled. "I really am sorry about all this, Annie. It won't happen again."

"No more hanging around with Brad when he's drinking?"

Steven's lips curled with disgust. "No way! He's a real jerk when he's drunk. Are—are you going to tell Dad?"

Anne sighed. "I might have to, Steven. But not until he gets back. If you've learned as much as I think you have tonight, then I'll make sure he doesn't come down on you too hard." She remembered Rob and grimaced. "I can't answer for Mr. MacNeil, though."

Steven's face fell. "Oh, yeah—Rob."

"If you want, you can go up to bed and I'll talk to him about it."

Steven shrugged and looked resigned. "I might as well get it over with."

"It doesn't bother you that—well, he's going to take it upon himself to lecture you?"

"Not really. I mean, Rob's okay...and Dad did warn me he'd asked him to keep an eye on things."

"But..." Anne sighed and shook her head. "Never mind." There was no point in letting Steven know how much she hated to have Rob involved. "I'm going to make myself a cup of tea. Would you mind clearing things up out here?"

"Sure. And Annie..." Steven came to her and gave her an awkward hug. "Thanks a lot."

Anne squeezed him back. "Anytime, kiddo."

It was over half an hour before Rob returned. Ignoring Anne, he sat down opposite Steven and leaned forward, resting his arms on his thighs.

"Well?"

Steven shrugged with an apologetic look. "I did a dumb thing," he admitted readily.

"That's for sure." Rob looked seriously at him. "And do you realize what the worst of it was?"

Steven shot a quick look toward Anne. "Uh, the drinking?"

"The fact that Brad was all set to drive himself and those kids home, drunk as he was. Do you realize how serious that is?"

"Yeah, I guess."

"That's not good enough, Steve. I want you to *know* it's wrong. Brad could very easily have lost control and killed everyone, maybe taken another car with him." His face had settled into hard lines and his eyes were bleak. "It's something I feel strongly about and I want you to promise me two things—that you will never drive after you've been drinking, and that if the person you rode with has been drinking you'll try to stop him and find another way home. Do I have your word on that?"

Steve nodded quickly. "Yeah, okay. Sure."

Rob saw the sincerity on his face.

"Good. Now what punishment did your aunt decide on?" He glanced briefly at Anne, his eyes impersonal.

Anne spoke, her voice cool. "I'm not going to punish him. He gave me his word it wouldn't happen again. That's all I need to hear."

"That's not good enough—and I'm sure Ken would agree with me." He looked at Steven. "You left your aunt stranded and came back here to party, without permission. You were drinking, too, weren't you?"

Steven hung his head. "I had a beer," he mumbled.

"Drinking doesn't make you grow up any faster, Steve," Rob said, his voice unexpectedly gentle. "Sooner or later it just makes a mess of everything. Don't get into that scene, okay?" He sat back in his chair. "Now I want you over at my place by eight o'clock tomorrow morning. I've got work for you."

Steve looked reluctant, but didn't object. "All right."

Part of Anne wanted to intervene, simply because it was Rob giving orders to her nephew and she really didn't feel it was any of his business. But she could see that Steven had responded positively to what Rob had said, and it had been good solid advice, nothing she could object to. And a couple of days' work wouldn't do him any harm, but would help to reinforce what he had learned tonight.

"Maybe you'd better get yourself off to bed, Steven," she said. "And knowing how wide-awake you are in the morning, you'd better set your alarm."

Steven nodded as he stood up. Unexpectedly he stooped as he passed Anne's chair and kissed her cheek. "'Night, Annie. And thanks. See ya in the morning, Rob," he added with a wave of his hand as he went into the house.

There was silence for a moment and then Rob asked, "Don't they ever call you 'Aunt Anne'?"

Surprised by the question, Anne shook her head. "They tried when they were little, but 'Aunt Anne' was a mouthful—it came out 'An-An'—eventually just 'Annie.' I don't mind."

She looked at him, her eyes alive with curiosity as she remembered how he had spoken to Steven about drinking and driving, as though the consequences were something he had experienced firsthand. Had he lost someone that way? That could explain the shading of pain she had glimpsed in his eyes. She felt a stirring of sympathy for him.

"I want to thank you for coming by," she said in a low voice. "I could have handled Steven and the others okay, but Brad..."

Rob looked at her coldly. "None of this would have happened if you had paid a bit more attention to the boys at the ballpark—and a little less to Boychuck."

"But Wayne and I are friends—the boys know that."

"So does half the damned town," he growled, standing abruptly. He glared at her again, then left, leaving her sitting in stunned silence.

Is that what he thought—that she and Wayne had something going on? That was ludicrous! But...if she thought about it, their behavior might be seen as flirtatious by someone who didn't know them, or realize just how much in love Wayne and Judy were.

Grinning widely, Anne leaned back in her chair. Was that what he really thought? It made sense—the first time he had met her, she and Wayne had been going at it in fine form. Rob would naturally feel sympathetic toward Judy and look upon Anne as the Jezebel leading Wayne astray. A low chuckle escaped her lips. She would have to straighten him out.

If he knew the truth, would he treat her differently? Did she want him to? Of course she did. It wasn't pleasant to see the dislike in his eyes every time he looked at her.

Anne sat in the warm night, staring up at the stars visible through the treetops. There was more to it than that, she knew. She wasn't going to try to pretend that the attraction she felt for him didn't enter into it. Such a strong physical reaction should be explored, she realized. Not by jumping into an affair, but by getting to know him, finding out what he was really like. Finding out if there was any substance to what she was feeling.

CHAPTER FIVE

THE HOUSE her grandmother had lived in was small, but suitable for Anne. All she really needed was a little space she could call her own and the chance to be independent, yet still near her family. She had lived away for too long to want much distance separating them.

It wasn't much more than a cottage, easily fifty years old, but still in good repair. True, the outside could use a coat of paint, as could the walls inside, but as Anne looked around, she realized that simple cosmetics would make the place into a comfortable home.

It was out of sight of the main house, nestled in a fold in the land on the other side of the little creek. Spruce trees grew tall around the perimeter of the yard and an ancient cottonwood had claimed the front lawn, its gnarled limbs reaching out toward the house. A swing hung from one of the branches and Anne sat on it for a moment, smiling as she remembered how she used to swing as a child while her grandmother sat on the veranda in her rocking chair.

Inside, there were four small rooms downstairs and a larger kitchen that had been brought up to fairly modern standards over the years. One of the few pieces of furniture remaining in the house was a big oak table and chairs. Anne had brought her good pieces with her from Toronto and was sure they would fit nicely into the house.

Steep stairs off the kitchen led to an attic room that had been partitioned into two bedrooms. A trickle of sweat formed on Anne's upper lip in the hot musty rooms as she looked around thoughtfully. *It'll be my winter project,* she thought, knowing she could turn the rooms into a single attractive bedroom. In the meantime, she could use one of the rooms downstairs.

Anne wandered around the house, making note of what supplies she would need. Wallpaper for the living room, she thought, and paint for the kitchen. A smile played across her face. She would like living here. It had been like a second home to her, growing up. She had spent many happy hours with her grandmother.

Anne knew it would be a good time for her to get started on cleaning the house, but it was easy to talk herself out of it. The sun was hot in a blue sky and the air was filled with soft, summer smells and the drone of busy insects. It was far too nice a day to get involved in serious housework. Anne stepped out onto the veranda and breathed deeply, ridding her lungs of the musty, closed-in smell of the house.

She walked over to the grove of spruce trees at the back of the yard. Here was another place she had played as a girl. The low, spreading branches and the cushion of needles beneath the trees had made a wonderful hideaway. She had spent hours there, breathing the heady, sun-heated scent of the needles and listening to secrets whispered by the branches in the gentle summer breezes, lost in worlds of her own imagining.

Something new had been added to the land just beyond the spruce trees. Here her father's land ended and Rob's began. A new gravel road led from the highway to his place. Curiosity led Anne on. She wanted to see the house he had built.

Although she would rather have avoided the openness of the road for the cover of the trees, Anne didn't trust her ankle to uneven ground. It had almost healed, but there was still a weakness and she knew it would be easy to turn it again. She walked slowly along the road, the sun beating down on her back, bared by the halter dress she was wearing. A dust devil swirled playfully before her, lifting dirt and leaves in its helter-skelter leap across the road. A red-tailed hawk caught the updraft and soared high above her.

The road curved around a rise in the land, back toward the river. Anne remembered the spot well. It, too, had been a favorite place of hers, from which she had been able to see the Spirit Hills.

As she finished rounding the curve, she could see them again in the distance and stopped to look. The Spirit Hills were the remnants of an ancient delta where the Assiniboine River had flowed into glacial Lake Agassiz thousands of years earlier. Giant dunes of shifting, windblown sand covered the area, stabilized in places by spruce, juniper and tamarack. It was often referred to as the Carberry Desert, and Anne knew that in places a low-lying cactus grew, and that there was a rare lizard, the northern prairie skink. It was a unique and special land, a place Indians had long revered, now protected as a provincial park.

As Anne continued down the road, she could see that Rob had built his house near the spot where she had spent hours dreaming as a girl. Even at a distance, she could see it was a lovely house. She had to concede that Rob had read the setting well and built accordingly.

The buildings didn't dominate the land, but blended in with appealing harmony. The house, with its peaked cedar roof and gleaming windows, seemed to flow with the rise of the land. The barn and outbuildings of gray weathered wood didn't seem too new or out of place, and the pastures were fenced with rough, unpainted logs. The setting, with its surrounding trees, looked perfect. Anne loved it.

She left the road and went to the pasture farthest from the house to lean against the fence, spending a few minutes just looking around. With a sigh that contained more than a bit of regret that the land couldn't be hers, Anne turned to go. Rather than follow the road back, she decided to cut across the pasture and take the path that led along the riverbank. It would be a cooler, more pleasant way back than the dusty road. If she went slowly, there should be no problem, she decided, tired of pandering to her ankle. Ducking, she climbed through the fence.

There were two horses in the far corner and as Anne got closer, she recognized one of them as Cinnabar, the mare Rob had been riding the day she'd sprained her ankle. The mare raised her head from the grass and watched Anne approach, ears cocked in curiosity. Anne smiled and detoured so that she would pass closer to the animal, calling out softly as she came nearer.

The other horse paid no attention, standing with its legs splayed and head hanging, shudders rippling across its body. It made no attempt to move as Anne stopped in front of it, frowning in consternation. Something was obviously wrong.

She's pregnant, Anne realized, seeing the swollen, barrellike sides. As another shudder rippled through the mare, it became apparent that she was in labor. Anne stroked her velvet muzzle softly, wondering what she should do.

She had grown up on a farm, but it had been a grain farm. Aside from the ponies she and Ken had had as children, she'd had little experience with livestock. Did the mare need help foaling, or could she manage on her own, as nature had originally intended? The mare stretched out her neck and nickered and Anne was sure she heard distress in the sound.

Anne couldn't stand there and do nothing. She grasped the mare's halter and started to lead her toward the house and barn. The horse took a couple of steps, then balked, refusing to go any farther. Anne tugged on the halter, to no avail. Another shudder coursed through the big body.

"Okay, girl," Anne murmured. "I'll go get help." She gave the horse another pat and turned toward the house, feeling as though she should hurry, yet fearing too fast a pace could cause her ankle to twist again. She stopped and looked at Cinnabar standing nearby.

She held out a hand, moving closer. As she reached for the halter, the mare lowered her head, nuzzling at Anne's shoulder. Laughing, Anne petted the chestnut neck. "How about it, girl? Will you let me ride?"

She was doubtful she could control the animal without even a lead rope. Still, she had to try. Carefully she climbed onto the fence rail and grasped a handful of Cinnabar's mane, easing a leg across the broad back.

She had no way to guide the mare, but she hoped that, like most horses, Cinnabar would head willingly to the barn. Tentatively Anne dug her heels into the horse's sides and the animal obligingly began to move. Encouraged, Anne tried a little harder and made a clucking noise with her tongue.

"C'mon, girl. I can walk faster than this. Let's go." Anne leaned forward as the mare quickened her pace to a trot. To Anne's relief, her leg muscles tightened automatically, balancing her against the jostling movement. She hadn't forgotten how to ride. Leaning forward until she was almost parallel to the mare's neck, she tightened her knees. "Atta girl—let's go!"

Cinnabar's pace quickened, became smoother and Anne felt a thrill of exhilaration as they clattered toward the gate at the end of the pasture. Her skirt and hair flared behind her, and for a brief moment she was one with the horse. It had been a long time, and it felt great.

Unexpectedly the gate was open. Anne sat up as they approached, slowing the mare's pace as they went through the gate into the yard. Rob appeared suddenly from the house, ran quickly down the stairs and stood with his hands on his hips, frowning.

Cinnabar stopped just in front of Rob with a little whinny.

"Just what the hell do you think you're playing at?" he demanded, reaching for the halter.

Her cheeks flushed with heat and excitement, Anne glared back at him. "I thought you might like to know you've got a mare in labor out there." She jerked a thumb in the direction she had come from.

Rob's look was one of total surprise. "Ruby? Are you sure? It usually happens at night."

Anne slid off Cinnabar's back and stood before Rob, carefully rearranging her skirt. "I'll admit I don't know much about it—and I certainly don't know if it's Ruby or not—but there is another horse at the far end of the pasture and she's obviously with foal. And distressed. I think you should go check it out," she added, a little miffed that he didn't seem to believe her.

Rob swore softly under his breath. "She's supposed to be in the corral beside the barn." He turned on his heel and went to check.

Anne watched him go, making a face at his back. "That's gratitude for you," she muttered to herself.

She stroked the side of Cinnabar's head. "Thanks for the ride, girl," she murmured with a smile. "It was great. Maybe we can do it again sometime." She started to walk away.

"Anne. Wait."

Anne turned around as Rob came out of the barn.

"She's gone, all right," he said. "The gates were left open. I'll have to go bring her back."

"I tried to lead her in, but she wouldn't come. I really think she's close to having it, Rob."

Rob nodded. "I'll go phone the vet. Could you stay?" he asked unexpectedly. "Archie's gone into town for supplies. I might need your help."

"I don't know that I'll be much use," Anne said. "But I'll do what I can."

"Good. Put Cinnabar into the corral for me while I phone. Please," he added as a definite afterthought as he turned to go to the house.

Anne took Cinnabar by the halter and led her to the corral. "I see your master is his usual charming self," she said to the mare as she turned her loose. Carefully closing the gate behind her, she went up toward the house.

Rob was on the phone when she came up the back stairs. Spotting her through the screen door, he gestured for her to enter.

Anne opened the door and stepped into the coolness of the kitchen, looking around with appreciation. It was a very modern room, spacious and bright, done in almond accented with Wedgwood blue. The countertops were tiled and the cupboards were of streamlined blond wood, as was the large table near a wide bow window. Anne stood beside the door, waiting for Rob to finish on the phone, staring back at the huge marmalade tabby cat regarding her coolly through unblinking yellow eyes from its position on a stool under a window.

"The vet's out on another call," he told her as he hung up.

"So, what do we do?" Anne asked.

"Become midwives," Rob said with a sudden smile that softened his face attractively. "You up to it?"

"Does it get gory?" she asked, wrinkling her nose.

"A bit," he said, laugh lines crinkling the skin around his eyes.

"I'll try not to faint." She held up her hands and shrugged. "Let's do it."

ROB DROVE HIS TRUCK across the pasture to where Anne had seen the mare. The horse had moved into the farthest corner and stood with her head down, looking utterly forlorn and dejected.

"Poor thing," Anne said as they got out of the truck.

Rob was frowning. "She looks tired," he said, going swiftly to the mare. "What's the matter, lass?" he spoke softly, soothingly, as he stroked her nose and ran a hand along her shuddering side.

"Come hold her halter, Anne. I want to take a look."

Anne obligingly held the mare's head steady while Rob did a quick examination. "How is she?"

Rob wiped his hands on a burlap sack he had brought with him from the truck. "About to give birth," he said.

Anne's eyes widened with dismay. "Do you know what to do?" she asked.

Rob shrugged. "Basically. My father is a vet. I used to follow him on his rounds when I was a kid and help him out whenever I could. Anyway, I think Ruby can do most of it on her own. She just needs a bit of support."

He cupped the mare's muzzle in one hand and stroked her strong, arching neck with the other. "Eh, lassie," he crooned softly, his accent becoming more pronounced, "we'll see you through this. Don't worry now."

Anne watched him soothe the restless horse with his softly spoken words. She found herself glad that she had stumbled across the mare, not only for the animal's well-being, but because it would give her a chance to get to know Rob. She had decided she wanted that.

She hadn't seen him since the night after the ball game almost a week ago. Steven had gone to work for him, spending three days helping his hired hand, Archie, cut and bale alfalfa. To Anne's surprise, Rob had paid Steven for his labor. Steven hadn't expected it, either, and had sung Rob's praises to Anne almost nonstop. Instead of irritating Anne, it had made her curious. She wanted to see why everyone seemed to hold Rob in such high regard.

Rob looked at her suddenly, catching her soft gaze on him. He returned the look for a moment, their eyes meeting cautiously. Anne looked away first.

"How long do you think this'll take?" she asked lightly.

Rob shook his head. "It's hard to tell. I hope not long. Why—do you have to be somewhere?"

She shook her head quickly. "No, the boys are both busy today. Steven went swimming with some of his friends. Not Brad," she added quickly. "I think he's given up on him."

"And what about Scott?"

"Don't worry, I haven't lost him," she said, arching her brows over cool eyes. "He's spending the day with Kris Wilson."

"He spends a lot of time there, doesn't he?"

Anne couldn't help but resent his tone. "He and Kris are best friends. They like to spend a lot of time together."

"They could be spending it at your place." There was a hint of accusation in his voice.

Anne was glaring openly at him by now. "Really, Rob MacNeil, none of this is any of your business. But if you must know, they're in the middle of building a tree house out behind Kris's house. That's why Scott is over there so often. It's not because I'm trying to get rid of him."

Rob started to say something, but Anne interrupted. "Stop paying so much attention to my affairs, which are none of your concern, and look after your horse."

For a second Rob's eyes turned cold, but a little nicker of distress from the mare turned his attention instantly from Anne. She was relieved. It was obvious his opinion of her hadn't improved much over the past few days.

"Hold her halter again," Rob said abruptly. "I think she's about to deliver."

Anne quickly took the halter, making soothing noises to the mare as Rob went around to her hindquarters. The mare grunted and strained, her head drooping to the grass. With another grunt, she lowered herself onto the grass.

"C'mon, Ruby girl," Anne murmured. "You can do it."

"It's coming," Rob said. "That's a lass—give it another push." His hands closed around the foal struggling to emerge from its mother's womb and pulled gently as the mare strained again. "That's done it," he said. "One more push. Come on, lassie." With one final rippling shudder, Ruby expelled her foal into Rob's hands.

Quickly the mare was back on her feet. "Let her see it, Anne," Rob said, standing back. There was excitement mingled with satisfaction in his voice.

The mare needed no bidding. Nickering deep in her throat, she snuffled the foal as it lay wet and blinking on the sun-warm grass.

Anne knelt beside Rob, her eyes shining with excitement. "It's beautiful," she said softly, awe in her voice.

"A filly," Rob said. "And a beauty." He reached over and rubbed a hand across Ruby's nuzzling muzzle. "Good lass," he murmured.

The foal was trying gamely to get to its feet, but its long, delicate legs refused to cooperate. Ruby whinnied soft encouragement.

"Poor baby," Anne said. "Can't we help her?"

"She'll do it soon," Rob said, but then got up and slipped a gentle, helping hand under the foal, steadying it on its feet. It stood, giving a bewildered little toss of its head that nearly sent it down again. "Take it easy, little one," Rob said, laughing. "Go see mama."

Anne marveled at the foal's unerring instinct as it pushed tentatively at the mare's udder, seeking the bond of warm, rich milk.

"Isn't nature remarkable? She knew exactly what to do."

"Programmed like the finest computer," Rob agreed, then laughed at Anne's expression. "No, I agree. It's nothing short of miraculous. It amazes and thrills me each time I see it." His smile for her was unexpectedly open and warm.

Anne responded to that smile, her own lighting her face with a radiance that caused his eyes to turn serious as they examined her closely. She looked away quickly, feeling something stir deep within.

"What do we do now?" she asked, keeping her voice level.

Rob sat down on the ground beside her, using the burlap to clean his hands. "We'll give them a few minutes," he answered, "and then get them back to the barn. I don't want them spending the night out in the open."

"Can she walk that far yet?" Anne asked, indicating the foal. It was on the ground again, knobby legs folded underneath as its mother nuzzled it softly, her breath blowing in the stiff, pale chestnut mane.

"She'll be off and running in no time. But we'll take her in the truck. You can hold her in the back."

"Do you think Ruby will mind if I pet her now?"

Rob shook his head. "I don't think so."

Kneeling, her skirt flaring over the ground, Anne leaned forward, delicately touching the tiny, pale pink muzzle. "It's the color of wild roses," she said, delighting in the velvety softness. "Like a rosebud."

Rob, sitting cross-legged on the ground beside her, smiled lazily. "You've just given her a name, Anne."

Anne turned to him. "Rosebud?" she asked doubtfully.

"Why not? Not her official name, of course. Her pet name."

"I guess we can always call her 'Rose'—or 'Rosie.'" She ran a finger over the white star between the foal's wide, brown eyes. "She sure is a beautiful little thing." Leaning back, she glanced at Rob. "Do you just have Ruby and Cinnabar?"

"So far. I'll be buying another mare in the fall and breeding Cinnabar soon."

Anne sat back, arranging her skirt carefully over her knees. "So you're a breeder."

"Not in a big way. It's more of a hobby. Basically I just wanted to keep a few horses around, and I like the looks of the Arabian. They're a bit small for riding. At least," he amended, "for me. But they've got a lot of spirit. I like that."

It was pleasant to have him talk to her in normal tones, without the underlying dislike and heavy-lidded, disapproving glares. She felt surprisingly at ease in his company and enjoyed listening to him.

"How long have you been in Canada?" she inquired.

"What gave me away?" he asked, turning to her.

Anne laughed. "I think it was something like 'poor wee lass,'" she teased, imitating his accent.

Rob's eyes crinkled at the corners and he smiled. "I tried so hard to drop the accent," he admitted. "I was fourteen when we emigrated. The last thing I wanted was to sound different from anyone else."

"I like it," Anne said lightly. "Tell me, where did you end up?"

"Just outside of Vancouver. Dad bought into a practice right in the middle of dairy country."

"Was it hard for you?" Anne asked. It couldn't have been easy for a boy that age to leave everything for a new country.

"It was for a while," Rob answered. "But it wasn't long before I couldn't imagine living anywhere else."

"So what are you doing on the prairies? Most people from the coast can't live without mountains in their backyard, never mind survive our winters."

His eyes darkened and she saw a cold bleakness in them before he turned away. "It suits me here," he said briefly, getting lithely to his feet. "It's time we got back."

Anne got up, brushing off her skirt as she looked at him, wondering what sadness had marred his life. It was sadness she sensed in him; she was sure of it. Would she ever know him well enough to find out?

Rob squatted beside the foal and lifted it gently into his arms, then carried it to the truck, closely followed by Ruby, her ears pricked anxiously.

Rob turned to Anne when he reached the truck. "Put the tailgate down," he ordered. "You can sit on it and hold her. I'll go slowly. Ruby will follow."

Anne did what he asked, too caught up in her own thoughts to resent his demanding tone. She sat and took the foal in her arms, resting its head and shoulders across her lap. She looked at Rob, her blue eyes wide and serious; the return of his remoteness disturbed her.

He turned away. "Hang on tight," he said, opening the driver's door. He got in and started the engine, driving off slowly. With a nervous whinny, Ruby followed.

Anne held the warm body of the foal closely, not caring that its coat was still damp from birth. The truck dipped suddenly as they crawled across the uneven pasture and she tightened her grasp as she squirmed back a bit. The mare followed closely, her nose almost touching the tailgate in her anxiety to be as close as possible to her baby.

"Just a few more minutes, Ruby," Anne said soothingly. "Then she's all yours." She glanced over her shoulder, looking at Rob's broad back through the rear window, thinking of his withdrawal.

It seemed different this time, not the dislike she had sensed before. She wouldn't take it personally, but would act as though it hadn't happened. She liked the Rob MacNeil she had sat and talked to today. She wanted to know more about him.

ROB STOPPED THE TRUCK in front of the barn and came around to the back, lifting the foal from Anne's arms. Anne smiled at him as she stood up, brushing off her skirt.

"That wasn't so bad," she said. "Although I think Ruby was bothered."

"I'll get them into the barn," Rob said. "Once they're settled, I'll see that they're left alone for a bit. She'll calm down once she has her baby all to herself."

The barn, though new and immaculately clean, had the warm, musty smell of all barns. Dust motes reflected sunlight streaming in through the open doorway. Anne sneezed as she followed Rob inside.

He turned and looked at her. "Allergies?"

Anne shook her head. "The dust tickles my nose." She stood aside as Ruby crowded in behind her.

Rob put the foal on a bed of straw in one of the stalls. It lay for a moment, round eyes blinking, then struggled to its feet. Ungainly and tottering, yet showing unmistakable signs of grace to come, it snuffled at Ruby's flank until it found the warm udder. As it suckled, its tiny tail wagged in contentment.

Anne stood back with Rob watching, feeling very conscious of the big, silent man beside her. Something inside wanted very much to be able to reach him. She looked at him and smiled.

"I feel as though I should thank you," she said, impulsively laying a hand on his arm. She removed it quickly as she felt him stiffen.

"For what?"

She rubbed fingers that still tingled with awareness of the crisp dark hair on his arm. "For being a part of all this," she answered, keeping her voice steady. "It was quite an experience. I never saw anything like it before."

"Well, I have. And it never seems to lose any of the magic. There's something special about birth."

"It's the reassurance, I think. That life will go on." Anne thought of Judy and the expression of contentment on her face as she cupped protective hands around her swollen womb. "It must be wonderful to experience it," she said softly.

Rob turned abruptly on his heel and walked away. "I'll get washed up and then drive you back," he said with a brief look over his shoulder.

Anne sighed, following him out of the barn. *Here we go again,* she said to herself. *What did I say* this *time?* "I could stand a wash myself," she said, catching up to him.

"Of course."

The bathroom Rob showed her to was upstairs, off the master bedroom. It was spotlessly clean, decorated in gray and red. As she washed her hands and arms, Anne looked at herself in the mirror with a grimace, thinking that she looked decidedly grubby. Her hair was windblown and there was a streak of dirt across the front of her dress. She splashed water over her face, dried off, then tried to smooth her hair, but without a comb there wasn't much she could do. Giving up, she looked toward the door leading to Rob's bedroom. It was partially open, and she gave in to curiosity.

Cautiously poking her head around the door, she peered inside. It was large, with a gray carpet and simple furniture with clean lines. There was a king-size bed with a deep blue comforter, positioned to look out of floor-to-ceiling windows. French doors on one side led to a small balcony. Anne knew the view would be of the river and the distant, beige dunes of the Spirit Hills.

On the wall opposite the bed was a collection of photographs, shots of sunsets. They were good, Anne realized after a quick glance, but they didn't tell her anything about Rob. There was a silver-framed picture on the dresser near the bed, but without going into the room, Anne wasn't able to see it clearly. Curious as she was, she wasn't going to risk Rob catching her in his room. She returned to the bathroom and left by the doorway leading out into the hall.

The staircase was open, with a simple, highly varnished railing of oak. Anne ran her fingers along the smooth surface as she descended into the living room, looking around appreciatively. The room was large and bright, with the same type of windows she had seen in the bedroom. There was a large stone fireplace with a raised hearth. A soft-looking, overstuffed couch sat invitingly before it, and there were two armchairs that could be pulled closer to the fire. Enlarged nature photographs were arranged in attractive groupings around the room.

There was a dining area next to the swinging doors that led to the kitchen, but instead of the expected table, there was a large desk holding a word processor and piled with paper. It was the only spot in the house that wasn't immaculate. Anne looked at the desk as she reached the bottom stair, wondering what task Rob did there. Was it just an office area where he kept track of records and accounts? Somehow she didn't think so. The untidy stacks of paper and overflowing wastepaper basket made it look as though he used it a lot.

She glanced up to see Rob standing in the kitchen doorway. "Are you a writer?" she asked with a disarming smile. Her mother had always said, "If you want to know something, ask."

His answering smile held an unexpected trace of self-consciousness. "I'm trying to be."

Anne was intrigued. "What are you working on?"

"Nothing too elaborate. I'm combining some pictures I took with text—nature books."

"Can I see the pictures?" she asked impulsively.

"Sure," he said with a shrug. Going to the desk, he rummaged under a pile of papers, finding a folder that he held out to her. "Here."

Anne opened it, exclaiming in delight at the photographs inside. They were of a family of coyotes and had been taken locally, judging from the landscape. There were four energetic cubs and a weary-looking, somewhat bedraggled mother. The pictures were very appealing. "These are good, Rob. Where did you take them?"

"Back in the hills, about three miles from here. I stumbled across the den early this spring, before the snow was gone. I was able to sneak up on them a few times when the wind was right. When I saw the prints, I thought I should do something with them."

"Are you writing a story, or just sticking to the facts about coyotes?"

"It's a kids' story. I'll keep it accurate, of course."

Anne finished leafing through the photographs and handed back the folder. "Well, I think it's a great idea. There's a lot of demand in schools for books like that. If this one works out, you should consider a series."

"I already have," Rob confessed. "There's a lot of wildlife in this area. It's just a matter of being in the right place at the right time. With a camera," he added.

Anne studied his face for a moment. He was handsome enough when he was cold and remote, but his softened visage was even more attractive to her. She looked away when his eyes met hers. "I should be getting back," she said. "The boys will be home for supper soon."

"I'll drive you." He pushed the kitchen door open and held it for her. Anne's shoulder brushed against his chest as she walked past him, and she felt a little tingle run down her arm. When she looked up, she saw her awareness reflected in his eyes before he moved away. *I'm about to get it bad,* she thought. The surprising thing was, she didn't really care.

Anne was thoughtful during the short ride home. She had learned a bit more about Rob today, but still didn't know much about him. Not about his personal life, anyway. His character was becoming more apparent to her each time she saw him, and much in his manner interested her. She had seen evidence of his gentleness and patience, as well as glimpses of a sense of humor. Those were qualities she admired in a man.

Evident too was the magnetism of his strong, vibrant masculinity. Part of her cautioned that she should put a damper on her feelings, but somehow she felt safe. She was certain this man wasn't going to rush her into anything. Quite the contrary. While he might be aware of her, it was basically in a negative way. And although he might feel some spark of attraction, he wasn't about to act on it.

Anne sensed he had suffered greatly, lost a part of himself to some sorrow that had yet to heal. The expression on his face when he'd talked to Steven about drinking and driving made her wonder if he'd lost someone under those circumstances. That would explain the shadows she had glimpsed in those topaz eyes.

AS THEY ROUNDED THE CURVE in the driveway, Anne saw there was another car parked by the house.

"That's the Boychucks' car," she said, opening the door of the truck as Rob pulled to a stop. It must be Wayne, she thought, doubting that Judy would be going very far from home these days. "Thanks for the ride home, Rob."

As she spoke, Wayne came from the back of the house. "There you are, Annie," he said in his deep, jovial voice. "I thought I'd find you baking beside the pool. Rob, how's it going?"

Rob didn't answer, merely gave a curt nod of acknowledgment, his face still and dark. "Thanks for your help this afternoon," he said briefly to Anne. As she shut the cab door, he immediately backed down the driveway and drove off.

Wayne ran a hand through his thinning hair. "What's with him, Annie. You been giving him a hard time?"

Anne's thoughtful look turned into a smile as she watched the truck disappear around the bend in the road. "I suspect the man thinks we're fooling around, Boychuck."

Wayne's answering look of surprise was comical. "You and me!" He made a face. "That would be—"

"Darned close to incestuous," Anne finished for him with a laugh. "You're beaming from ear to ear, Wayne, and I know it isn't my company. What is it—boy or girl?"

Wayne's chest puffed with pride. "One absolutely beautiful baby girl. Born just before noon today."

"And?" Anne prompted.

"And what?"

"How much did she weigh, what's her name, how's Judy doing... minor details like that."

"Offer me a beer and I'll fill you in."

Anne seated Wayne beside the pool and made a quick trip to the kitchen to get him a bottle of beer. He accepted it with a smile of thanks and took a long swallow.

"Ah," he said. "After gallons of hospital coffee, this tastes like ambrosia."

"You always say that. Okay, make like a proud father and tell me all about it. First, how's Judy?"

"A little tired, but healthy and happy. It was quite something, Annie. I saw the whole thing, got to hold the baby right away." He shook his head, his eyes shining with awe. "It was beautiful. Anyway, the baby is perfectly okay. She weighs eight and a half pounds." He grinned. "The nurses call her 'Chubby Cheeks.'"

"I'm so glad everything is okay, Wayne. I know how worried you were. I can't wait to see her."

"Go tomorrow," Wayne said. He took another swallow of beer. "The family is piling in today. Oh, by the way, we want you to be godmother."

Anne smiled, pleased with the honor. "Oh, Wayne. That's a lovely thought. Thank you." She sat back in her lawn chair. "So, does this kid of yours have a name?"

"Lindsey Anne," Wayne said. "We decided to stick your name on the end in memory of the many good times we've all had together."

"Thank you, Wayne," Anne said, genuinely touched. "That means a lot to me."

"I figure you'll feel obligated to baby-sit now," Wayne said, grinning.

"I should have known there was a catch," Anne told him, sighing. "Oh, well... It just so happens I'd love to, anytime."

"It'll be a while yet, I'm sure." He glanced at his watch. "I gotta get going. I told Judy I'd be back around suppertime."

Anne stood up with him. "Thanks for coming by to tell me. And let Judy know I'll be in tomorrow afternoon, early. Is there anything she needs?"

"Just someone to ooh and ahh over the baby."

Anne laughed. "That won't be a problem. I can hardly wait to visit them. See you," she called as Wayne left.

Anne sat back down, smiling with pleasure, glad everything had worked out so well for Wayne and Judy.

As she sat, her thoughts once again turned to Rob. She remembered the look on his face and the speed with which he had left after seeing Wayne.

A smile played softly about her face. Now she was quite sure that Rob did think she and Wayne had something going on, and that was the reason for his dislike. She would definitely have to set him straight.

CHAPTER SIX

ANNE DROVE a reluctant Scott and Steven to Brandon to stay with Margo's parents. Anne understood how they felt, leaving their friends and summer activities, but stressed to them how much the visit would mean to their grandparents. That they doted on the boys was immediately obvious, and Anne knew the two were in for three weeks of spoiling and indulgence. After joining them for a light lunch, Anne left to do some shopping.

She took advantage of the trip into the city to get the supplies she needed to begin work on her grandmother's house. She had been putting it off, hating the thought of confining herself while the days were so bright and beautiful. But it was about time she got started, so she could move in before her parents got back from England. With the supplies packed in her car, Anne drove home.

It was far too quiet in the house. Anne had become used to having the boys around, and missed the almost constant noise that seemed to follow them. There was no stereo blaring, no phone ringing, no queries about what was for supper. She wished that Ken and Margo hadn't arranged for the boys to go to Brandon. It would have suited her to have them in her care for the entire six weeks.

Anne felt restless after supper, in spite of the distance she had driven that day, and decided to go for a walk. Without really thinking about it, she headed toward Rob's.

It was early evening, and the sun was low but still strong. Small, puffy, white clouds with sharply planed gray bottoms drifted across a powder-blue sky. Anne followed the path along the riverbank, stopping for a moment to listen to the bell-like trill of a meadowlark.

As she came in sight of Rob's place she hesitated, thinking that maybe she should turn around and head for home, but she really wanted a chance to talk to him, hoping to get an opportunity to let him know how wrong he was about her and Wayne. Deciding she could use the excuse that she wanted to ask about Ruby and her foal, Anne continued toward the house, determined to follow through.

He was sitting out on the deck, the dog at his feet. The big orange cat she had seen inside the house the other day lolled in a corner planter, crushing the flowers. Anne had to smile. For a man who usually seemed so stern and distant to her, he apparently was a real softy as far as his pets were concerned.

Blue spotted her, gave a little woof, then was on his feet, wagging his way toward her. Anne laughed at his exuberant welcome, then glanced tentatively at Rob.

"Hi," she said. "I hope you don't mind. I thought I'd come over and see how Ruby and the baby are doing."

He surprised her with a lazy smile of welcome. "I was just having a cup of coffee," he said. "Would you like some?"

Anne climbed up onto the deck and sat down on a redwood lounge chair. "Yes, please," she said with a smile. "I take it with a bit of milk," she added as he got up lithely and went to the house.

He was back in a moment, handing her a mug of aromatic coffee.

"Thanks," she murmured. She took a sip as he sat back down.

"I take it the boys are all settled at their grandparents'?" Rob had talked to Scott and Steven before they had left that morning.

Anne nodded. "I wish Ken and Margo hadn't arranged all this. I would have liked to have them stay with me the whole time. But Margo's parents seemed awfully glad to have them. It'll probably be the last chance they get to be with the boys like this. They may come home spoiled rotten, though."

"It won't last," Rob said assuredly. "They're good kids."

Anne smiled in agreement. "They are, aren't they?" She watched as the cat got up from his begonia bed, stretched and yawned before jumping down onto the deck to come and investigate Anne. He gave her ankle a somewhat haughty sniff, submitted condescendingly to a pat, then walked off, striped tail held high.

"What's his name?" she asked.

"Big Red."

"It suits him." She tilted her head and glanced at Rob, her eyes lighting with laughter. "I would have thought that was *your* nickname, though," she teased.

He shook his head. "They stuck me with another one."

"What? Come on," she coaxed, when he hesitated. "You heard mine the other night." She made a face. "What could be worse than 'Stork'?"

He looked at her, his face relaxed and smiling. "Try 'Big Mac.'"

Anne's clear, lilting laugh echoed in the still air. "That's pretty bad, all right. But 'Stork' was worse."

"Maybe. Certainly a misnomer." His assessing eyes swept quickly over her.

Anne caught the intensity of that look. "Not when I was fifteen," she said, feeling her heartbeat quicken. She shifted in her chair and took another drink of coffee. When she looked at him again, his face had settled back into impassive lines, and that brief look might never have been.

He put down his cup and stood. "Let's go see the horses." He went quickly down the steps, the dog at his heels.

Anne followed slowly, thinking. He was attracted to her—she was sure of it. But he didn't want to be. Was it just because he thought she and Wayne had something going on?

Once she cleared that up, what would happen? What did she want to happen? Anne looked at him, seeing his bare, muscular legs beneath old, cutoff jeans, appreciating his masculine grace and strong good looks. Physically she had no doubts as to what she wanted, but she refused to give that unreasoning, primitive core credence. Blind, physical reaction only led to trouble.

She followed Rob around the barn to the corral at the side. Ruby was there, her foal pressed close to her flank.

Anne joined Rob, leaning against the fence. "Look at her! Isn't she a little beauty? And all ready to run." Seeing them, the foal put her head down and gave a little running buck. Anne laughed and looked. "Were you serious about calling her 'Rosebud'?"

"We've been calling her 'Rosie.'" He chuckled. "Archie thinks it's a ridiculous name for a horse, but it seems to suit her. And she is on the red side."

"Like everything else around here," Anne noted. "All the animals seem to be one shade of red or another." She grinned at him. "Even you. You should get married and produce a couple of redheaded kids to complete the picture."

The stone-cold mask that dropped over Rob's face told her instantly she had said something wrong.

Anne frowned in concern. "What is it?"

Rob shook his head. "Nothing." His tone was as masked as his face.

Anne touched his arm briefly, hating the sudden coldness in his voice. "Something I said upset you, Rob. I'd like to know what it was."

He turned to her with icy eyes. "I had a son," he said harshly. "He and his mother are dead. Is that what you want to know?" Without giving her a chance to respond, he strode away.

Her eyes wide with horror, Anne watched him go. When he disappeared inside the house, she left, walking home slowly, knowing there was nothing she could have said to him that would help ease his pain. And he was in pain. She had seen it in his eyes, heard it in the bleakness of his voice. He had lost two people he loved.

How had it happened? Somehow she knew it must be related to the talk he had given Steven about drinking and driving. He'd had the same look on his face then. Had he been the one drinking? Anne felt a shudder go through her. What horror that would be for him. She hoped it hadn't happened that way. The guilt would be unbearable.

Subdued, Anne let herself into the house. She had gone over to his place this evening with the intention of correcting his mistaken ideas about her relationship with Wayne. It seemed so unimportant now.

She poured herself a glass of orange juice and took it outside. As she sat watching the sun slowly set to the chirr of crickets, she pondered how little she knew about Rob. Their encounters hadn't always been overly friendly, but there was something about him she liked.

She had been piqued because he had shown so little interest in her, amused when she realized that he thought she had something going on with Wayne. Her ego had wanted his masculine attention, she admitted to herself. She wasn't used to being ignored by men, whether she chose to respond to them or not. But after tonight she knew that Wayne or no Wayne, he wouldn't have been interested in her. He was a man in mourning.

She had wondered earlier what it was she wanted from Rob. She knew now. It was quite simple, really. She wanted to be his friend.

ANNE COULDN'T SLEEP. Her bedroom was hot and close, even with the window open wide. Finally she gave up tossing and turning, trying to find a cool spot on the pillow, and got up. She pulled on her bathing suit and made her way downstairs in the dark. A quick swim would cool her off and help her to sleep.

The night was very calm. Moon shadows stretched over the deck and the silver light reflected in the water. Anne sat on the edge of the pool, slowly submerging her legs. The water felt quite cool and she began to think maybe she didn't want a swim, after all.

A sudden movement from the far end of the deck caught her eye. Her head shot up and a startled gasp escaped her lips.

"It's all right, Anne. It's me, Rob."

Anne breathed a loud sigh of relief as she heard the quick, reassuring words. "You scared me."

"I'm sorry." He came toward her, a dark, looming form. "I came for a swim. I know it's late, but I didn't think you'd still be up." As he came closer, the moon lit his craggy face.

"It's all right. And you don't have to leave," she added as he picked up his towel. "Stay and have your swim." She saw his hesitation and added with a smile in her voice, "And I won't even mind if you don't."

He hung his towel over one of the chairs and sat down beside her, lowering his legs into the water. "It's colder than I thought it would be. I might change my mind."

"I was thinking along those lines myself." She felt the water stir against her calves as he moved his legs back and forth. She glanced past his bare chest and shoulders to his face. "Rob... I'm sorry about your loss." She had to say something.

He gave an abrupt, accepting nod. "I want to apologize for the way I acted earlier," he said, his deep voice gruff.

"Oh, Rob, it's all right." She touched his arm, her sympathy reflected in her eyes as she looked at him. "What was your son's name?" The question was impulsive. As she sensed his sudden tension, she wished the words unspoken.

"Jamie." He spoke softly. "He wasn't even three, Anne. But he was a great little guy...."

Tears welled in Anne's eyes and she bit at her lip to keep them from spilling over. She heard the love, the yearning in his voice. "How long has it been?"

"Just under three years—a little bit longer than Jamie was allowed to live." The harshness was back in his voice.

"What happened?"

"A drunken driver slammed into their car. Lisa—Lisa was killed instantly. Jamie lived for two days." There was a world of pain underlying the stark words.

"I'm so sorry, Rob." Anne's voice throbbed with sympathy. The words seemed so inadequate. Nothing she could say would ease the pain this man had suffered.

Rob ran a hand through his hair and sighed. "I didn't come over here to lay this on you, Anne."

"I know...but I don't mind." She glanced at him and changed the subject. "Do you still want that swim, or have you decided the water is too cold?"

Blue chose that moment to appear. Tongue lolling, he galloped across the deck, pushed himself between Anne and Rob and launched himself into the pool. They were drenched by a cold spray of water.

Laughter bubbled from Anne, joined by Rob's rich chuckle. What a great tension breaker, Anne thought with relief as the dog swam excitedly about their legs.

"Well, the decision has been made for me." Anne pushed herself into the pool and turned over to float on her back. "Come on in. It's not bad after a minute."

Rob stood, ducked his head between outstretched arms and dove in over her, surfacing several feet away. Blue let out a yelp of excitement and paddled madly toward his master.

The water felt deliciously cool against Anne's skin once she got over the initial shock and she swam slowly across the pool, watching Rob at play with the dog. He had pushed the pain away, but she knew it must be an ever-present feeling, one that could surface at any time. How long would it take for such wounds to heal?

Blue gave up trying to catch Rob and turned to Anne. She moved quickly to avoid his paws. "You great goofy mutt," she admonished, swimming away. "Are you trying to drown me?"

"He'll drown himself in a moment," Rob said. "He doesn't know when to give up." He swam to the shallow end and stood on the cement steps. "Blue—here, boy. Time to get out." The dog, head held high, paddled toward him and hauled himself out of the water. He pranced around for a moment, gave his fur a violent shake, then plopped down, panting rapidly.

Anne trod water, watching Rob's sleek head glistening in the moonlight as he swam several fast lengths, his arms cutting through the water with powerful strokes. When he finally finished and pulled himself out of the pool, Anne got out, too.

She watched as Rob dried his face and arms with the towel he had left draped over one of the lounge chairs. Tilting her head, she wrung water from her hair, lifting it from where it was plastered to the skin just above the swell of her breasts. She wished she had brought a towel from the house. The air that had seemed so warm before her dip in the pool now felt cold against her wet skin. Shivering a bit, she rubbed her arms.

"Cold?" Rob asked.

Anne nodded. "I should be able to sleep now. It was the heat that kept me awake."

"I ought to be going." He slung the towel over his shoulders and pushed his feet into his moccasins.

"Did you walk over?" she asked.

"I usually do. It's a nice distance for a walk. Ready, Blue?"

"Rob, wait." Anne walked toward him as he turned around to look at her. "I'm having Wayne and Judy over for supper tomorrow—with the baby, of course. Would you like to join us?" She saw his hesitation, knew he was about to refuse.

She spoke quickly. "I think I should tell you...well, I got the impression that you think Wayne and I are—are having an affair or something." She made a little face and laughed at the thought. "We're not. We just tease a lot."

She stood, waiting for a response, very aware of his presence, of the heat emanating from his body. She wanted so much to step closer to him, allow his lips to capture hers. Did he know?

He knew.

His dark eyes looked at her and Anne could feel them linger on every moonlit curve. She ran a tongue over lips suddenly dry.

"Will you come?" she asked again, striving to keep her voice level. "We'd love to have you."

"All right," he said abruptly. "What time?"

"Anytime after four. We'll eat early. They won't want to be out late with the baby."

"See you then." He turned on his heel and walked away, the dog trotting behind him.

Anne stood and watched him go. Her breath was coming a little faster than normal and her pulse was quick.

She had been wrong about wanting Rob to be her friend. She wanted to be much more than that to him.

ANNE GOT EVERYTHING ready early. She had picked lettuce from the garden and left it crisping in the fridge. There were tiny new potatoes waiting to be boiled with a sprig of mint. She had shelled the first of the peas and pulled up baby carrots to steam, and there were steaks for the barbecue.

She showered and dressed in a summery blue dress, sleeveless with a scooped neckline and flowing skirt. Her hair was loose, caught back on one side with a mother-of-pearl comb, and she wore just a touch of makeup to emphasize her eyes.

Finished her preparations, she took a book and her glasses out to the yard to lie on the hammock stretched between two basswood trees. The trees were covered with tiny white blossoms that emitted a lovely, sweet scent. Anne breathed deeply and stared up into the sky for a moment before opening her book. What could be more wonderful than the hot, heady days of a prairie summer? Pushing her glasses up on her nose, she opened her book and began to read.

It was so peaceful, so quiet. Lulled by the heat and the incessant drone of insects, she couldn't stop her eyelids from flickering shut, and she dozed off.

A fly tickled her nose. With a sleepy murmur, she brushed it away. It came back again and she opened her eyes in annoyance. Rob stood beside the hammock, laughing down on her, a stalk of timothy grass in his hand. He drew it across her nose again.

"Caught you napping," he teased.

Anne stretched a little, causing the hammock to sway gently. Pushing her glasses into place, she smiled, appreciating Rob's light mood. He seemed so much younger, more approachable. "Are you early, or did I sleep too long?"

Rob lowered himself to the ground beside the hammock. "I'm early." He looked at her closely, a smile playing across his face. "I like the glasses. They make you look like a schoolteacher. What are you reading?"

Anne picked up the book. "It's about the experiences of some of the early pioneer women in Manitoba. Fascinating, really. I don't know how they did it. The hardships were incredible."

Rob's eyebrows raised slightly. "And here I thought you were into some fluff with a titillating title like *Passion's Desire*."

Anne pushed up her glasses and grinned. "That was last week. I'm into actual histories at the moment. I enjoy them. They give us a real insight into our past."

"Now you sound like a teacher."

Didn't he know? "I *am* a teacher."

"You are?" There was surprise in his voice. "Ken told me you were a model."

"Only part-time—while I went to university." She sat up carefully in the hammock, dropping her legs over the side. "I'm a history teacher. I'll be teaching at the high school in September."

"Then this isn't just a holiday."

Anne shook her head. "I'm here for a year or two, maybe longer. Didn't Ken tell you?"

Rob shrugged. "Not that I recall." His eyes were thoughtful as he looked at her swaying gently in the hammock, the tips of her toes brushing the grass. "It seems I've had a few misconceptions about you."

"Meaning I'm not an empty-headed hussy bent on seducing my best friend's husband?" She said the words lightly, a teasing gleam in her eyes.

Rob chuckled. "Something like that."

She cocked her head and smiled at him, holding out her hand. "Then can we be friends now?"

He raised his shoulders and shrugged, his lips curving into an attractive smile as his fingers closed warmly around hers. "I don't see why not."

"Good." Their eyes met and she saw curiosity in his before he released her hand. Things had changed between them, and she was glad.

She slid out of the hammock and picked up her book. "I have to finish getting dinner ready. Wayne and Judy will be here soon."

"I'll give you a hand," Rob said, getting to his feet. He followed her to the house, his brow etched with a thoughtful frown.

"GREAT STEAK," Wayne said, cutting into his piece with relish.

"Thanks," Rob said.

Anne shook her head in exasperation. "Typical male," she said to Judy. "All he did was slap the meat on the barbecue and turn it over when it started to smoke. I got everything ready, and he takes the credit."

"There's a fine art to barbecuing steak," Rob said.

"Something women can't seem to get the hang of," Wayne agreed around a mouthful of food.

Judy made a face at her husband. "Oink, oink. You should have fed them pork chops, Anne."

"That's a good idea," Anne said with a laugh. "But wouldn't that be cannibalism?"

"It would, come to think of it," Judy giggled. She was looking slim and happy, an aura of contentment about her. She glanced often at the baby sleeping in a car seat in the shade of her chair.

"How has Lindsey been?" Anne asked, changing the subject.

"Wonderful," Judy answered. "She's just perfect." She glanced again at her sleeping daughter. "She's even considerate enough to let me sit through a meal."

"That won't last," Rob said. "Babies develop a kind of radar sense after a while. They seem to know when you don't want to be interrupted and decide that's a good time to demand attention."

Anne watched him as he spoke, wondering what memories he was recalling, but nothing showed on his face. He seemed relaxed and at ease. Anne was glad he wasn't brooding about the past. She was enjoying his company. His presence added a lot to the evening.

Judy insisted on helping clear up, over Anne's protestations.

"I haven't been allowed to do a thing for the past two weeks," she said, gathering plates from the table. "The guys can keep an eye on the baby. Let's get this done with, then we can relax with a cup of coffee."

As soon as they were alone in the kitchen, she turned to Anne. "You and Rob seem to be getting along fine. Been getting to know each other, have you?"

"A little," Anne said lightly. "He is our closest neighbor, after all. And Ken did ask him to keep an eye on things while he and Margo were gone."

"I'm surprised you went for that. The Anne I know would have told Rob to mind his own business."

"I did, a couple of times. But then I decided he wasn't so bad."

"That's an understatement!" Judy turned from stacking plates in the dishwasher. "So—do I sense romance?"

Anne shook her head quickly. "No, no. Nothing like that."

"Why—aren't you interested?"

Anne wrapped leftovers for the fridge. "You sound like Margo."

"And you're avoiding the question. Are you interested?" Judy repeated, grinning widely at the look on Anne's face.

"Exactly like Margo," Anne said with a sigh. "I guess you could say I'm interested. But that's as far as it goes at the moment. Don't make anything out of it."

"What about him? Is he coming onto you yet?"

"No, he's not. And that suits me just fine, Judy." She could tell Judy about his wife and son and put an end to the questions, but she felt it was something Rob wouldn't want repeated.

"Well, I guess it's early in the game yet. But don't leave it too long to make your play, Anne." She flashed a wide grin. "Not only is he handsome, he's taller than you. You won't find too many more around here like that."

"I don't care if a man is shorter than me."

"But *they* do."

"True," Anne said with a nod, remembering how Graham had hated her to wear heels that would make her seem just a little bit taller than he was. She had the feeling that something like that wouldn't bother Rob, though. He was confident of his masculinity.

"We're finished in here," she said. "I'll take the coffee. You grab the dessert."

"Mmm—strawberry shortcake."

"What else? I've been overrun with strawberries."

They took the coffee and dessert out to the deck. Wayne was in the pool, floating on his back. Rob sat on one of the lounge chairs, the baby nestled in the crook of his arm. He smiled at them.

"She got restless as soon as Wayne hit the water," he told Judy. "She's developing that radar right on schedule."

"She must be getting hungry. It's been a while since her last feeding."

Rob jiggled his arm as the baby made a little sound and gently wiped a bubble of spit from her lips. "Are you nursing?" he asked easily.

Judy nodded, taking the chair beside Rob. She leaned over, smiling at her daughter. "Look at that face." She laughed as the baby frowned in concentration. "She's trying to figure out who you are, Rob."

"Uh-uh," Wayne said, coming from the pool. "I've seen that look before." He wiped his face with a towel. "It's diaper-duty time."

Rob held up the baby. "She's all yours, Dad."

Wayne scooped up his daughter in his big hands. "Come here, Princess," he crooned. "I'll make you comfy."

Anne grinned in delight, watching the ease with which Wayne diapered his daughter and changed the sleeper she was wearing for a dry one. She glanced at Rob and knew that he, too, had been a nurturing father. Holding the baby had obviously been pleasurable for him and she was glad his memories weren't all filled with pain and a sense of loss.

"Here you go, Annie," Wayne said, handing her the baby unexpectedly.

Startled, Anne took the baby in arms that felt suddenly stiff and awkward. Gingerly she squirmed back in her chair, looking down on the tiny, scrunched-up face. The baby's eyes opened and she blinked, looking impossibly serious. Relaxing, Anne smiled and held her closer, enjoying the feel of the warm little body pressed against hers. When she looked up again, she saw the others watching her.

"It's nice," she murmured with a contented little smile, brushing a finger across the baby's fair, wispy hair. "You have a beautiful daughter," she said to Wayne and Judy.

Judy met Wayne's eyes and they shared a smile. "We do, don't we?" she said with deep satisfaction.

"You should get yourself one," Wayne drawled, his eyes taking on a teasing glint.

"One of these days," Anne agreed. Her eyes flickered across to where Rob sat, watching her. Looking back down on the baby, she couldn't help wonder who would father the children she wanted to have.

IT WAS STILL EARLY when Wayne and Judy decided to leave. Rob walked with Anne to the car to see them off.

"Thanks for coming, guys," Anne said. "I really enjoyed it."

"Thank you for having us," Judy replied. "The meal was great, and it was nice to get out for a while. I haven't been too far from home this past little while." She turned to flash her wide smile at Rob. "It was nice seeing you again. We'll have you over soon."

Rob returned her smile. "I'd like that, Judy."

"Don't forget, if you need a baby-sitter, call," Anne said.

"I think I'll call Rob," Wayne grinned. "He looked like he could handle things better than you."

"Thanks, Boychuck," Anne told him dryly. "I'll remember that when you're desperate."

"Oh, by the way, Anne," Judy said as she slid into the car. "There's a baseball windup Saturday night at the hall. Why don't you come?"

"I thought the picnic was the windup," Anne said.

"That was for the kids. We decided the adults needed something more. They'll be giving out awards, too."

"Yeah," Wayne said. "You'd better come and cheer for me, Annie. I'm taking the Most Valuable Player Award."

"What d'you do—stuff the ballot boxes?" Anne teased. "Anyway," she added, looking back at Judy, "don't you need me to baby-sit?"

"Mom's coming over," Judy said. "I *think* I trust her with Lindsey." She glanced over her shoulder at the baby in the back seat, then looked at the others, smiling a little sheepishly. "I hear it wears off eventually. If you do decide to come, Anne, bring a dish. It's a potluck supper."

"Call me later in the week. I'll let you know then."

"Will do. Talk to you later." Judy waved to them as Wayne backed down the driveway.

Anne turned to Rob. "Would you like another cup of coffee?" she asked.

Rob glanced at his watch. "One more, then I've got to get going."

They settled themselves on the deck with mugs of coffee.

"I really was wrong about you and Wayne, wasn't I?" Rob said unexpectedly.

A little surprised, Anne nodded. "As I said, we just tease a lot. Judy expects it as much as Wayne does." She looked at him curiously. "It really bothered you, Rob, didn't it?"

He nodded, looking down into his mug of coffee. "It reminded me of another situation." He glanced at her briefly. "One that wasn't so innocent."

"Someone you knew well?" she asked.

"My former partner, Jim," he said, then continued, "I counted him and his wife, Cathy, as my best friends—I'd known them for years."

"What happened?"

He shrugged. "We hired a new woman for the office, a receptionist who modeled on the side. She was nothing but a troublemaker. I could see it, but Jim was blinded by her blond hair and big, blue eyes." He caught the look on Anne's face and added, "Just a superficial resemblance—I can see that now." He smiled at her.

"Anyway, she went after Jim after she'd tried it on with me and got nowhere. I tried to talk some sense into him, but he wasn't listening. To cut a long and obvious story short, Cathy found out at one of the staff parties. Jim and the woman weren't even trying to hide it by that point. They left together, and I had to explain things to Cathy." He frowned at the memory.

"I lost a lot of respect for Jim during that time. I might have understood it if he'd been in love with Tanya, but it wasn't much more than lust, and nothing, not even Cathy and the kids, was going to stand in the way of what he wanted."

"Is he with her now?" Anne asked curiously.

Rob shook his head. "Those things never last. Tanya moved on to someone else once the excitement was gone, and Jim tried to get Cathy back. He honestly couldn't understand why she wouldn't have anything more to do with him."

"That certainly explains a few of the heavy-duty looks you gave me," Anne said teasingly. She put down her mug and looked at him sideways. "Are you sure you're finished comparing me to the likes of Tanya?"

Rob relaxed with a grin. "Absolutely," he said warmly.

"Good," Anne said lightly, but she felt her heartbeat quicken as her attraction grew just a little bit more.

Anne expected they would sit in relative silence after that while Rob finished his coffee, but he was responsive to her attempts to make conversation and they chatted easily.

"I've got two sisters and a brother," he said in answer to her question. "All married with a parcel of kids—I've got nine nieces and nephews."

"You must miss being near them. I know I missed Scott and Steven when I was in Toronto."

"Why did you decide to move back?"

Anne shrugged. "There were lots of reasons. But basically I realized one day that home wouldn't be here forever. I wanted to come back before everything changed—really changed."

Rob put down his empty mug. "Selling the land was a big change."

Anne glanced at him. "It took some getting used to," she admitted. "But the family is still together and we've still got the house and the land around it. That's the main thing." And it was. It didn't matter who owned the rest of it. "Tell me, why did you decide to move out here?"

"I like it here." He stared out into the gathering dusk for a moment and then spoke in a low voice. "I took my brother's motorcycle after the accident. I had to get away...the house was so cold and empty, my job meaningless." He took a deep breath and continued.

"I did a lot of traveling, took the back roads.... I camped at Spruce Woods one night, then decided to hike back into the Spirit Hills. I spent the night lying in the sand, staring up into the sky. I'd never seen a sky like that before. It was brilliant with stars. And then the coyotes started to sing. I felt..." He held up his hands, not knowing how to finish.

"A sense of peace," Anne finished for him, her voice soft with understanding; she hoped that some of his pain had been eased. "A night like that soothes the soul." She smiled a little self-consciously as he looked at her. "It was the first thing I did when I got back from Toronto."

He looked skeptical. "You camped out—by yourself?"

She had to laugh at the look on his face. "Hey, I'm tough. I love camping. Ken and I used to do it all the time when we were kids."

He was eyeing her thoughtfully. "You surprise me."

Good, she thought, but said nothing.

"I should be going," he said, glancing at his watch. He stood. "Thanks for the meal, Anne. It was enjoyable."

She stood beside him and smiled warmly. "Thanks for your help. And I'm glad you were able to come."

He gazed down at her, his eyes hooded as he studied her smiling face. "What are you doing tomorrow?" he asked abruptly.

Anne wrinkled her nose and sighed. "I've got to get some work done around here. The weeds in the garden are growing faster than the vegetables. If my mother saw it, she'd have a fit. And the lawn needs mowing. That's a job in itself." She tilted her head and looked up at him. "Why?"

His face relaxed and he smiled. "I was wondering if you'd like to go riding with me. Ruby's up to it, and Cinnabar needs a run."

"I'd love that, Rob."

"Well, let's make it in the early evening—say seven? It'll be cooler then, and I don't want your mother thinking I encouraged you to neglect your chores."

"You're scared of her, too, are you?"

Thinking of Lillian, Rob grinned. "Let's just say I'd like to keep on her good side. See you about seven, then?"

"I'll be there. Good night, Rob."

"'Night, Anne." He smiled and then he was gone.

Anne sat down. Leaning back in her chair, she stared up into the sky, thinking of Rob. A feeling of excitement welled up inside her and she jumped to her feet, hugging her arms to her chest.

She knew for certain tonight that Rob liked her, and it came as a surprise to know how much that meant to her. In a short time Rob had become important to her, and somehow it felt as though she had always known him. It hadn't been this way with Graham, she thought, realizing again just how much their relationship had been built on surface things. No wonder it hadn't lasted.

She took a deep breath of warm, perfumed air and looked about her. A pensive frown creased her forehead. *I think I'm falling in love,* she thought suddenly. Folding her arms across her chest, she began to pace the deck. What was that going to mean?

She had to assume that Rob had loved his wife, that he would still be married to her if fate hadn't decreed otherwise. How long did it take the heart to heal? Rob might be attracted to her... but was he ready to love again?

CHAPTER SEVEN

ANNE STARTED on the garden early, but it was already hot. Weeding was a chore she had hated as a child, and time hadn't made it any better. Some people loved to dig their hands into the soil, enjoyed pampering growing things. Anne wasn't one of them, although she did enjoy the results of a well-tended garden. Nothing tasted better than freshly picked vegetables.

She was hot and dirty by the time she finished the garden and there was still the lawn to cut. She was tempted to put it off until the next day, but had already decided she had to make a start on her grandmother's house. *Get it over with,* she told herself, trudging to the shed where the mower was kept. At least the old push mower she and Ken had taken turns using when they were growing up had been replaced by a little tractor. It made the task a lot easier.

The appearance of a freshly cut lawn was worth the effort. Wiping a hand across her sweaty brow, she gazed around with satisfaction when she had finished. It was late afternoon, but there was still time for a swim before she ate and got ready to go over to Rob's.

Rob had been on her mind throughout the mechanical tasks of the day. She was looking forward to seeing him with an intensity that worried her. If she felt this way after knowing him such a short time, what was seeing more of him going to do?

She cautioned herself not to expect too much from his invitation. It was highly unlikely that he was looking for romance at this point in his life. While she felt that he was attracted to her, she also sensed that it wasn't something he was ready to act upon. And in a way she was glad. With physical feelings put on hold, there was time to really get to know each other. She had come to realize just how important that was.

Anne showered, dried her hair into golden waves that she caught back with a scarf and applied makeup lightly. She dressed in thin, khaki-colored slacks and a short-sleeved blouse, an outfit that was comfortable and perfect for riding.

She glanced at the clock as she finished dressing. It was early, but she decided to leave, anyway.

She walked slowly toward Rob's place, taking the shaded path along the river. It was still hot, the air humid. Gray-bottomed clouds rimmed the horizon, their white tops piling into cottony peaks. She took a minute to watch the river, thinking again about what Rob's invitation might mean.

He probably just wants company, she thought. Or someone to help exercise his horses. She kicked a stone ahead of her as she walked on. Wishful thinking could be leading her to see something that wasn't there. The attraction she thought she sensed in him might just be a reflection of her own feelings. *Take it slow,* she warned herself. *Keep it friendly.*

Rob was out by the corral behind the barn. There was another man with him. Archie, Anne assumed. He was short, with hunched shoulders and a deeply tanned, lined face with brown, cocker-spaniel eyes. He wore denim overalls and an oil-stained cap with a cracked brim.

Rob waved her over. "Anne, this is Archie Macomber. Archie, this is Ken Hammond's sister, Anne."

Anne smiled and held out her hand. "Hello, Mr. Macomber. It's nice to meet you."

Archie took her hand briefly, nodded a greeting and turned back to saddling the horses. Anne sensed the shyness behind his taciturn manner.

"Are we taking Rosie?" she asked Rob.

"Ruby won't go far without her. She can keep up. We'll take it slow."

"I'm looking forward to this, Rob. I haven't had a real ride in years."

"Except for that little jaunt through the pasture you took on Cinnabar—bareback, with your skirt flying out behind you. You made quite a picture." He flashed a smile at her, then turned to tighten the cinch on Ruby's saddle.

Anne leaned against the fence, watching. The horses stamped their feet and flicked their tails against flies. The filly scampered about her mother, her long, knobby legs already quick and sure.

Rob was wearing jeans and a white cotton shirt with the sleeves rolled up over his arms and the top few buttons undone. Anne looked at him, feeling her attraction to him flutter deep within. *I can't help myself,* she thought ruefully.

Take it slow, she cautioned herself again. *Keep it friendly.*

"Where's Blue?" she asked, looking around for the dog. The marmalade cat was perched on a fence post, watching them, but there was no sign of the exuberant Irish setter.

"He's in the house," Rob said. "I'm taking my camera in case we come across any wildlife. With Blue along we won't see anything, unless it's a flash of tail with Blue in hot pursuit." He picked up the camera that had been hanging on a fence post and slung it over his shoulder. "Ready?" he asked Anne.

"Ready."

"We'll be an hour, maybe two, Archie. You can let Blue out later if you want."

"Right, Boss." Archie handed Cinnabar's reins to Anne and, with a shy, rather endearing smile, left in the direction of the barn.

"Get up on Cinnabar, Anne. I'll adjust the stirrup length for you."

Anne mounted, looking down on Rob's gleaming, russet hair as he shortened the stirrups a notch. She tightened her fingers on the saddle horn, resisting the temptation to stroke back the lock that curled over his forehead.

"Does Archie live in the house with you?" she asked.

"No, he bunks in a couple of rooms off the barn. It's better than it sounds," he added, seeing her look. "I got them fixed up so they're quite comfortable for him. There're kitchen facilities and indoor plumbing. From what he's told me, it's the best he's ever had. He's spent his life as a hired hand—living conditions were often quite primitive." He finished with the second stirrup and tugged it into place. "That should do."

Anne slid her feet into the stirrups and tested them. "Perfect. Thanks."

Rob nodded his response as he picked up Ruby's reins and mounted, swinging his long leg over the mare's back with ease. "Let's go." He made a clucking noise with his tongue and Ruby moved off. Cinnabar followed automatically.

With the saddle creaking beneath her, Anne guided Cinnabar along the trail, following Rob. Rosie trotted close to her mother's flank, her stubby, pale chestnut tail flicking. The pace was fairly slow in deference to the foal and Anne took the time to look around.

They were traveling away from the river. The land was basically flat, but rolled gently in places. Dark green stands of spruce dotted paler fields, as did clumps of yellow-petaled black-eyed Susans. Sweet clover perfumed the air, stirred by a warm breeze. Anne couldn't have imagined anything more perfect.

Rob glanced back. Anne smiled at him, enjoying his quick, answering smile. Once again, she was glad they had settled their differences. This Rob was a man she liked very much.

Rob led them down an old, overgrown road. Poplar saplings grew up between grass-filled ruts and trees closed in on either side. At the end of the road was a clearing and a log cabin with a caved-in roof. Windows, with shards of glass jutting from rotting frames, stared like ancient, knowing eyes.

Ken had taken Anne to the cabin many times when she was a child and he still had to keep an eye on her. He might have been a considerate older brother in many ways, but he hadn't been above inventing tales about the abandoned cabin. Anne remembered his stories about bloody murders and ghostly children searching for their parents. She had been terrified, yet fascinated, demanding more from him. He never failed to oblige.

Rob stopped and waited for Anne to catch up. "I thought there might be some deer feeding around the cabin," he said. "I've seen them here before. I was hoping for a few pictures. I—" He stopped and held up his hand. "Listen."

Anne heard the *put-put-purrr* of the ruffled grouse. The male bird made the drumlike sound by cupping its wings and rapidly beating them against the air.

"I'd like to get a few shots of that," Rob said.

"Have you tried?"

"I got one in a good position early one morning. The sun was just coming up and there was a misty background—and then Blue came charging out of the bush. I was ready to pay someone to take him off my hands after that."

Anne nudged her heels into Cinnabar's ribs until they were side by side with Ruby. "Not for long, I'll bet."

Rob grinned and shook his head. "No. As goofy as that dog is, he's nice to have around. Shall we head back now?"

"It might be a good idea. We seem to have stirred up the mosquitoes—" she hit at one that was biting her arm "—and they want dinner." She reined Cinnabar around to head back down the road.

They road alongside each other this time. Neither spoke. Words weren't needed to share the quiet beauty. Anne felt content. *I could never have shared this with Graham,* she thought. He didn't have the depth to appreciate such an experience. He only enjoyed social occasions, ones where he could be seen by people who counted in his profession.

Anne realized how little Graham had been in her thoughts lately. It only confirmed what she had started to believe before she left Toronto. She hadn't lost the man she loved—she'd had a narrow escape.

She glanced at Rob, her mind leaping ahead with possibilities. Then she frowned, putting a quick stop to her fantasies, knowing she could well be setting herself up for disappointment—for pain. *Enjoy the moment,* she told herself firmly.

Suddenly Rob reined to an abrupt stop. After a quick glance, Anne followed suit. Ahead, walking tentatively toward them, were two white-tailed deer and a half-grown fawn. There was a crosswind and the deer caught no warning scent.

Rob had his camera focused almost instantly, waiting as long as he dared before releasing the shutter. Hearing the click, the lead deer shot its head up alertly. A high-pitched warning whistle pierced the air and they were off, white tails flashing.

Rob snapped another picture. "Got 'em," he said with satisfaction, replacing the lens cap and slinging the camera back over his shoulder.

"Are these shots for another book?"

"I'm hoping to do another one—I've got more than enough deer shots already. All I need is an interested publisher."

"Have you tried for one yet?"

He glanced at her. "I've been in contact with one company about the book on coyotes. They're interested and want to see what I've got. I just might have a new career as a writer."

"Great! I hope it works out. Rob, tell me about what you did before you moved out here."

"I was in advertising in Vancouver, in partnership with Jim, the man I mentioned last night."

He jiggled the reins and clucked his tongue. The horses started moving again. "I found it too competitive and often inane, especially once the initial challenge was gone and we began to reach the goals we'd set. And after the accident—well, selling my share of the company was one of the best decisions I've made."

"Are you doing what you want now?"

He nodded. "It was always in the back of my mind—early retirement to a bit of land away from the city. Lisa and I planned for it." He looked ahead as he spoke, his voice even and without emotion. "She was an accountant before Jamie was born and she liked to play the stock market. She invested every spare penny we had. Quite successfully... we'd just about reached the point where we could start realizing our plans."

Anne heard the hollowness of shattered dreams in his words. "It must have been hard to go on," she said softly.

"It was. But I couldn't return to what we'd had and I couldn't keep running."

"So you settled here."

"It suits me," he said briefly.

"Even the winters?" she asked, grinning suddenly in an attempt to lighten the mood.

His teeth flashed white and he nodded. "Even the winters. In fact, the change of seasons is one of the things I like the best. It's not the same on the coast. It's a little greener or a little wetter from one season to the next. Nothing as dramatic as this country. And how can you really appreciate summer if you haven't waded through six-foot snowdrifts all winter?"

Anne absently wove Cinnabar's mane through her fingers, sitting easily in the creaking saddle. "I love summer here. I'd almost forgotten what it was like. All these wonderful scents, the birds and flowers, the way the wind touches your skin on a hot day..." She took a deep breath, her eyes half-closed. "It's all so sensuous."

She caught his piercing glance and smiled self-consciously before looking away.

"Can we gallop a bit?" she asked. "Ken and I always raced over this stretch. Not that I ever won. Sundae could never keep up with his horse.

"Sundae?"

Anne grinned. "My pony. She was a black-and-white pinto. I decided she looked like a chocolate sundae. I spent more time riding her than I did anything else. And then I grew—and grew. My legs practically dragged on the ground when I rode her. Dad finally convinced me to sell her. I haven't ridden much since." She tilted her head and looked at Rob. "So, can we gallop?"

"Go for it. I think I should bring Ruby in slower."

"You don't mind?"

"Of course not. I'll see you at the barn."

Anne needed no further bidding. She leaned forward and dug her heels into Cinnabar's sides. The mare shot ahead, racing for home, and Anne exulted in the powerful, thrusting motion of the horse beneath her.

Rob was nearly fifteen minutes behind them. By that time Anne had petted an exuberant Blue, unsaddled Cinnabar, laughingly watched her ungainly roll in the dust and then curried her smooth again. She grinned at Rob as he trotted into the corral.

"Slowpoke."

"Oh, yeah? We'll try it without Rosie next time. Then we'll see who the slowpoke is." He returned her smile with lazy charm.

For a moment Anne was lost to that smile and the way it softened his face. Once again she was keenly aware of her attraction to him. Concerned that it might show in her eyes, she knelt to pet the dog. For the moment it was enough to know there would be a next time.

ANNE SWALLOWED the last of her gin and tonic, rattling the ice cubes in the bottom of the tall, frosted glass.

"That was perfect. Thanks, Rob."

"Can I get you another one?"

Anne put the glass down on the patio table. "No, thanks. I should be going. It's almost dark."

"I'll drive you."

"That's all right. I'll walk."

"Are you sure? I don't mind driving you."

Anne smiled as she stood up. "It's a short walk and it's such a lovely evening. Thanks for letting me ride Cinnabar. I really enjoyed myself."

Rob got up from his chair. "I'll walk with you."

"You don't need to do that. I'll be all right on my own."

"I'm sure you will. But I wouldn't mind a bit of a walk." He snapped his fingers at Blue, who was lying on the grass off the deck. "Hey, Blue, want to go for a walk?"

The dog's ears perked, then he leaped up with a yelp of excitement, his tail wagging furiously.

"I guess I'm outnumbered," Anne said with a laugh. "Let's go." Hugging a feeling of pleasure to herself, she walked beside Rob along the graveled drive toward the road.

The whole evening had been very enjoyable, much more so than she had really expected. The ride had been fun, but more important than that was the pleasure Rob's company had given her. It had been so easy to talk to him as they sat on the deck, sipping their drinks in the lingering twilight. He had questioned her about the history of the area and listened closely, obviously interested in what she had to say. Anne appreciated that. Most people tuned out when history of any kind was mentioned.

"It's a beautiful night," she said softly.

"It is, but I'd say we're in for a storm within the next couple of days." The sky above them was clear, but clouds edged the horizon, lit by sullen flickers of heat lightning.

Night deepened from indigo to velvety black and starlight reflected from the road to light their way. From far away came a whippoorwill's ceaseless chant. Crickets chirred in the grasses along the ditch, stopping when the dog padded past. The darkness felt warm and intimate.

A longing grew in Anne. She wanted more than anything for Rob to take her into his arms and kiss her. Would the kiss match the magic of the night? She knew it would. Her loins tightened at the thought.

She could initiate the kiss. But...would it spoil things between them? That Rob had loved his wife deeply was obvious to Anne. It was also obvious he hadn't put that part of his life completely behind him. He might respond to her out of sexual need, but it wouldn't be enough. *Not nearly enough,* she thought with conviction, aware of how deep her feelings for Rob were becoming.

"Almost there."

Rob's deep voice startled her out of her thoughts.

They left the road and cut across the lawn toward the house. A yard light shone brightly from a pole beside the driveway.

"You didn't have to walk me all the way home."

"I enjoyed it. And I wanted to be sure you made it all right."

"What could possibly happen out here?" Anne glanced at him and laughed. "There are no muggers hiding behind a tree, waiting to jump me."

"But you could have hurt yourself walking alone in the dark—twisted your ankle, maybe." His eyes met hers teasingly.

"That only happens when I stand eyeball to eyeball with a galloping horse."

Rob's laugh was low and deep. "Doesn't it bother you going into that dark, empty house all alone, without even a dog for company?"

"It didn't until you put it that way. Be careful, Rob, or I'll have you checking out the basement and looking under beds."

He laughed again. "Did you at least lock the door before you left?"

"After living all those years in Toronto? Of course I did." She fished in the pocket of her slacks for the key and unlocked the door. Turning to Rob, she smiled openly. "Thank you, Rob. I enjoyed myself very much tonight." Wanting badly to feel his touch, she held out her hand. As his lean, hard fingers closed around hers, Anne felt an intense surge of the desire that had been building in her all evening. Quickly she lowered her eyes and started to pull her hand from his.

His fingers tightened briefly, then relaxed. "I enjoyed myself tonight, too, Anne." He smiled as she looked up. "We'll do it again—only next time, I'll race you back to the barn. And win, of course."

She tilted her head and grinned. "Fat chance. You'll eat my dust."

He raised his eyebrows. "Is that a challenge?"

"I'd hardly call it a challenge," she teased, her eyes alight with laughter. "You wouldn't stand a chance."

"We'll see about that. Soon."

"I'll look forward to it."

He hesitated, then turned to go. "Good night."

"Good night," Anne echoed softly, and smiled, watching him disappear into the night.

JUDY CALLED Friday night.

"So, are you coming to the baseball social tomorrow night?"

"I don't know, Judy. I don't feel in the mood for that kind of thing."

"You'll enjoy it when you get there. Besides, you don't have to stay late. I won't. Tell you what. Come for the supper, then you can drive me home. Wayne's helping to run the thing, so he'll have to stay late, and I know I won't want to, but I would like to go for a while. How about it? C'mon, Anne," she coaxed. "Say yes."

Anne gave in with a laugh. "All right. But only for the supper. I don't want to stay for the dance."

"Not even if Rob's there?" Judy teased, laughing when Anne made no reply. "Okay, see you there about six. I'll save a place for you."

Anne replaced the receiver slowly. Judy's words had evoked a picture in Anne's mind. She could see herself dancing with Rob, being held in his arms as she moved with him to the music. Would he dance with the ease and masculine grace with which he walked? She knew he would. A delicious shiver of anticipation ran through her. She hoped he would be there.

ANNE DRESSED CAREFULLY for the evening, choosing a white cotton dress stamped with a black pattern. It tied around her neck, leaving her back bare, and the skirt flared from a belted waist, swirling about her knees when she moved. She brushed her hair into gleaming, sun-streaked waves and applied a touch of makeup.

It took her just over ten minutes to drive to the hall, and as she stepped into the interior, with its noisy buzz of conversation, she looked around, trying to find Wayne and Judy.

Judy spotted her and waved. "Over here, Anne."

Anne made her way to the table, carefully carrying a foil-wrapped pan.

"What did you make?" Judy asked.

"Sweet-and-sour meatballs," Anne replied. "What do I do with them?"

"Use 'em for tennis," Wayne piped up, grinning at the identical looks of exasperation he received.

"Ignore him," Judy said. "Hard as it is. Take them over to the kitchen. Some of the older ladies have volunteered to serve."

Anne made a quick trip to the kitchen and returned to take a seat opposite Judy. Wayne had gone to talk to someone at another table.

"He's not here yet," Judy said in a low voice, seeing how Anne's eyes darted around the room.

For a second Anne considered pretending she didn't know what Judy meant, then she shrugged and smiled ruefully. "Am I that obvious?"

Judy shook her head. "A lot of it's wishful thinking on my part," she admitted. "I'd love to have you and Rob fall in love. That way you might stick around for more than a couple of years. Just think, our kids could be best friends the way we were." She leaned across the table. "How *do* you feel about him, Anne?"

Anne looked down at her hands and rubbed a thumb across her nails. "I'm not sure, Judy. I like him—more than like him," she admitted. She looked up, a flash of concern darkening her eyes.

Judy caught the look and frowned. "Why should that bother you?"

Anne hesitated. The crowded hall was not the place for a conversation as personal as this. "Let's discuss it later," she said. It would feel good to be able to talk it over with someone.

ALTHOUGH JUDY HAD PLANNED to leave soon after the dinner and subsequent awards, Wayne talked her into staying longer.

"At least for a couple of dances," he'd added to his argument. "Lindsey is perfectly fine with your mother."

"I suppose," Judy admitted, giving in.

Anne half listened to their conversation. She had spent most of the evening watching the doorway, hoping to see Rob. It was hard to hide her disappointment as it became increasingly obvious that he wasn't going to show.

The dance started with a blast of old-time rock and roll. Wayne smiled blissfully and began snapping his fingers to the beat. Judy looked at Anne and raised her eyebrows. There would be no holding him back.

He pushed his chair back from the table and stood. "C'mon, girls," he demanded. "Let's dance."

"Both of us?" Anne asked.

Wayne shrugged. "Since you can't get your own man, I guess I'll have to take you both on. Besides, Judy won't dance if you're sitting here all by yourself."

"It won't be the first time we've done it," Judy said to Anne as she got to her feet. "C'mon Anne. Knowing you, you're dying to dance."

At some other time that might have been true, but tonight she felt deflated, let down. She had wanted so much to see Rob. Still, dancing would be better than sitting by herself. She stood and moved to join Wayne and Judy on the dance floor. They were just one of several groups of dancers. Nobody was overly concerned about having a partner.

Rob appeared before the second song was over. Sitting on the edge of a table close to where they were dancing, he folded his arms against his chest.

"I might have known I'd find the two prettiest women in the room with you," he said to Wayne.

Wayne grinned. "Someone's got to keep 'em happy. But I'm in a generous mood tonight. You can have one."

Rob winked at Judy and turned to Anne. "How about this one?"

"Good choice. I was hoping someone would take her off my hands." His grin grew even wider as Anne scowled at him, then he grabbed Judy and whirled her away with a flourish.

Anne slowly placed her hand in the one Rob held out to her, feeling his fingers close around hers. Her lashes swept down, then up again as she met his eyes.

"Hi," she said, her smile echoing the pleasure she felt.

He returned her smile warmly. "Hi. You look very beautiful tonight," he added, his thumb stroking her knuckles as he talked.

"Thank you." She felt tongue-tied and breathless, overwhelmingly aware of him and the touch of his hand on hers.

"Dance with me," he commanded softly as a song with a supple beat began to play. His fingers tightened on hers and he pulled her closer.

Resting a hand on his shoulder, Anne began to dance, letting the music flow over her as she joined with the rhythm of his body.

"I'm glad you decided to come," she said, looking up at him.

"I wasn't sure I was going to. But," he added, "I'm glad I did." His hands tightened as he twirled Anne around.

Dancing had always been very pleasurable for Anne, but until she danced with Rob, she'd had no idea just how sensual it could feel. The subtle touch of his body against hers was slowly arousing. Feeling warm and liquid, she had to fight to keep from melting against him, from letting him see just how much she wanted him. A glance showed his face as set and almost stern... but his eyes sparked as they met hers.

As the music slowed, Rob pulled her closer against him. Anne knew from the way he held her, from the way his body moved against hers, that he felt the undercurrents of desire flowing between them. With a little sigh, she gave in to what she was feeling and relaxed against him. He exhaled sharply, stirring her hair with his breath. She caught the heated, male scent of his body and breathed deeply, all her senses tingling with awareness. She knew then just how much she wanted Rob.

It took a lot of strength to push away from him, but she did, afraid of revealing too much. Her steps faltered and she stopped.

"I—I'd like to sit down," she said, a lock of hair hiding her face as she looked away from him.

Rob caught her chin between his thumb and forefinger, gently turning her face. "Anne, I—"

She pulled away from him with a little shake of her head. She had known she was attracted to him, but it came as a shock to realize just how strong, how intense that attraction was. Even now, in spite of all the people dancing around them, she wanted nothing more than to feel the crush of his lips against hers. And she knew that if they were alone, she would never be able to stop with just a kiss.

She gave him a quick, apologetic look over her shoulder as she made her way back to the table and sat down. He stood beside the table, gazing down at her, his face settled and his eyes impassive. Looking at him gave her no clue to what he was feeling, but she knew instinctively that her feelings were returned, at least in part.

"Can I get you a drink?" he asked abruptly.

"Please—just ice water," she added as he moved away. "I'm driving Judy home shortly." She watched him walk toward the bar, her eyes lingering on him. She had never known before how intense a physical attraction could be.

Her feelings for Rob, both physical and emotional, were growing at a rapid, almost uncomfortable pace.

Judy appeared suddenly at her side. "I can drive myself home," she said, sitting down. "Wayne can always get a ride with someone else."

Anne shook her head quickly. "I'll take you."

Judy looked surprised. "Are you sure? I thought you'd want to stay, now that Rob was here." She grinned. "Or after that dance, leave... with Rob."

Anne managed a brief smile. "No, I'm ready to go whenever you are."

Judy looked at her closely for a moment and then nodded. "It'll have to be soon," she said, glancing down at the bodice of her red cotton dress. "I'm going to be bursting out at the seams if I don't feed Lindsey." She stood. "Well, if you're sure you want to leave..."

"I am."

"Then I'll go tell Wayne. Be back in a minute."

As she left in search of Wayne, Rob came back. He put a glass of water down in front of Anne, then took the chair Judy had vacated.

Feeling more in control again, Anne took a drink of water. "Thanks," she murmured. "I was thirsty."

"Are you leaving?" he asked.

Anne nodded, rubbing a finger around the rim of her glass. "Judy wants to get back to the baby, and Wayne has to stay. I promised I'd drive her home."

"Anne..."

She looked up cautiously. "What?"

He reached across the table and took her hand in his, his face relaxing in a warm, open smile. "I enjoyed dancing with you."

Anne returned the smile, her eyes lighting with pleasure. "Me, too," she murmured, wondering if he had any idea just how much.

Judy was back at the table, looking at them closely. "Anne, if you'd like to stay..."

Anne shook her head quickly, pulling her hand away from Rob's. "I'm ready," she said, standing up. "Did you say goodbye to that husband of yours?"

Judy nodded. "And warned him to behave himself—although he's already requested a polka."

Anne laughed. "Then we'd better leave before he drags one of us out there to dance with him. Wayne is dangerous when he polkas." She looked at Rob. "See you," she said, her voice suddenly husky.

"See you," he echoed as she turned to leave, and she wondered about that next meeting.

ANNE CURLED UP in the corner of the couch in the Boychucks' living room, tucking her feet under her. She sipped a cup of tea while Judy settled into an armchair, the baby nestled in her arms.

"That's Lindsey taken care of," Judy said. "Now what about you, Anne?"

"I'm fine—this Earl Grey was just what I needed."

"That's not what I meant and you know it. I want to know about you and Rob."

"We're friends, that's all," Anne equivocated. She took another sip of her tea.

Judy gave a little snort of disbelief. "Right. Friends don't dance the way you two did, unless they're hoping to become more than friends. C'mon, Anne...talk to me."

Anne put down her cup and sighed. It would feel good to talk about it. "I'm very attracted to Rob," she stated, rubbing a finger along the seam on the back of the couch. "And—and I think he feels something for me." She looked up and caught Judy's eye. "But he's a widower, Judy. His wife and son died in a car accident less than three years ago."

Judy gave a little shudder, her arms instinctively tightening around her sleeping daughter. "What a nightmare that must have been for him."

Anne nodded. "It must have been hell. It still must be at times. How long does it take to get over something like that?"

Judy glanced at the picture of her and Wayne on the mantel and then down at the baby in her arms. "I'm not sure I ever would," she said quietly.

They sat in thoughtful silence for a moment, then Judy asked. "How far has it gone, Anne?"

"Not far at all," Anne admitted. "I know he considers me a friend—we get along quite well on that level. But there are undercurrents, Judy. I'm not naive. I know when a man is attracted to me."

"And that's not enough?"

"Not nearly enough—not with Rob."

"Are you in love with him?"

Anne caught her bottom lip between her teeth and nodded slowly, her eyes troubled. "I think I am." She raised the palms of her hands in a helpless gesture and added honestly, "Who am I trying to kid? I know I am."

Judy stroked a wisp of hair from her daughter's forehead. "If you want my advice..."

"I certainly do."

"Take it slow. Don't let things get out of control. He probably hasn't had a whole lot to do with women since his wife died. A lot of what he's feeling could just be—well, physical urges. He might be able to handle an affair at this point, but beyond that—" She shrugged.

"I want more than an affair," Anne stated quietly.

"Then don't sleep with him," Judy said bluntly. "It'll only complicate things. If he is going to fall in love with you, it'll take time, I'm sure. And if he's not," she added gently, "well, then maybe you won't get hurt as much."

Anne gave a tired smile. "Since when did you get so wise?"

"It's not wisdom—just empathy." Judy's eyes flickered again to the picture on the mantel. "It's not hard to imagine what he must have gone through."

CHAPTER EIGHT

ANNE WAS WELL INTO cleaning her grandmother's house, when she heard someone pull up in the driveway. She was glad of the interruption. Even with all the windows open, it was still hot and musty inside. Pulling off her rubber gloves, she wiped a hand across her sweaty brow and went to the door to see who it was. Rob was getting out of his truck. Her stomach gave a queer little flip and she hoped fervently that her inner feelings wouldn't show.

He grinned when he saw her and raised a hand in greeting. "Hard at work, I see."

Anne grimaced as she flopped down on the top stair of the veranda. "I hate housework. Especially in houses that haven't been cleaned in years. I'm sure there are mutant spiders lurking in there somewhere. You should see the size of some of those webs."

Rob stood gazing up at her from the walk, a foot on the bottom step, his eyes laughing. "You look hot and bothered."

Anne pushed back a strand of hair that was sticking to her damp face and straightened the shoulders of the old T-shirt she wore over cutoff jeans. "I am hot and bothered," she said with a growl in her voice.

"And cranky," he teased.

"Borderline. I haven't kicked the mop bucket across the floor yet." She smiled, enjoying his rich chuckle.

"You're obviously not cleaning because you think it's a fun thing to do. Are you moving in?"

She nodded. "Although I'm having second thoughts—make that thirty-second."

"You don't want to live with your folks?"

"My mother would drive me crazy with all her fussing. Much as I love her, I need a bit of distance. Besides, I've lived on my own for almost ten years. I'm used to my privacy."

Rob glanced at his watch and straightened. "I've got a couple of errands to run in town. Can I get you anything?" His eyes creased with laughter. "Cleansers? A new scrub brush . . . a fly swatter for those mutant spiders?"

Anne made a little face at him. "Go run your errands. Leave me to my labors."

Unexpectedly Rob reached out and with a soft touch pulled something from her hair. Anne's heart skipped a beat. He seemed so close and yet not nearly close enough. Her eyes flickered to his mouth, then away again as she stilled errant thoughts.

"What was it?" she asked lightly.

He grinned. "I'm not sure you want to know—you still have to go back in there . . . unprotected."

She wrinkled her nose at him. "Thanks a lot."

Still smiling, he turned to leave, then stopped and looked back at her. "Listen, you're obviously not going to feel like cooking after all this. Why don't you come over for supper tonight?"

Her eyes lit with pleasure. "Who's cooking?"

"I am."

"I guess I can risk it," she said with a casualness she didn't feel. "What time?"

"Around six?"

"All right. See you then." This time her smile was openly pleased. She raised a hand in answer to Rob's wave and watched him walk to his truck, appreciative as always of his lean, masculine grace.

She sat, her expression slowly growing troubled as he drove out of sight. She did love him; she was sure of it...but how did he feel about her? Friendship tempered with attraction—she could be sure of little else. But would it grow, become the love she needed—or was he caught in the past, loving the family he would never see again? With a sigh, Anne stood up and returned reluctantly to her chores. Only time would give her the answer.

A SHOWER WASHED AWAY the afternoon's grime. Anne dried her hair and left it loose, to tumble about her shoulders in sun-streaked waves. She wore a simple blue cotton halter-top dress printed with tiny white flowers, and flat white sandals on her bare feet. She looked cool, summery and pretty.

Her thoughtful mood had lightened somewhat. Nothing could completely quench the glowing core of excitement that flared each time she thought of Rob.

She took the river path to his place, walking slowly to stay cool. It was very hot and the humidity grew as thunderclouds pushed belligerently across the sky. Cliff swallows darted in the air currents above the river, snapping up insects for their demanding broods.

Rob saw her coming from the deck and raised a hand in welcome. Blue bounded down the steps and greeted her enthusiastically. Even the cat came forward and bumped against her legs.

"What a welcome," Anne said, laughing as she climbed the steps.

"I told them they couldn't eat until you got here," Rob teased. He was standing by the barbecue, dressed in khaki shorts and a white, short-sleeved cotton shirt. He looked her over as she approached, his eyes sharp with appreciation. "Well, you certainly cleaned up nicely."

"Thanks, I think. What's for supper?"

"Shish kebab—steak and marinated mushrooms. And tiny potatoes, new green beans and baby carrots, all straight from the garden. But first—" he picked up a frosted pitcher and poured into a salt-rimmed glass "—the perfect summer drink, a margarita."

Anne took the glass from him and tasted the drink. "Mmm—perfect is right. Thank you, Rob."

"I figured it would take care of any lingering effects from all that cleaning you did today."

Anne took another sip. "It's working. I feel all my troubles washing away." She sat in one of the patio chairs in the shade of the house and smiled. "I'm starving."

"Good. We'll eat soon. The coals are almost ready." He took the chair opposite hers, stretching his long legs out in front of him.

"Will Archie be joining us?"

Rob shook his head. "Archie prefers to get his own meals. Besides, he's off into town for a night of carousing. I book him into the local hotel when he goes on one of these nights. Not that it happens often, which is just as well. Archie's idea of a good time means downing beer until he can hardly stand, never mind drive."

"Poor old guy," Anne said. "It sounds as though he's had a lonely life."

"He has, from what I gather. But he seems happy enough working here. He likes the horses, and there isn't a lot of heavy work. He'd be lost in a retirement home, and at his age that's the only alternative."

Rob got up to check the coals. "They're ready. I'll go get the food."

"Need any help?"

Rob shook his head as he slid open the patio door. "Just sit back and relax."

Anne did just that, sipping slowly on her drink, looking out over the river toward the Spirit Hills. Cloud shadows chased over the land and a mourning dove crooned from a nearby tree. She smiled contentedly. She couldn't imagine any place she'd rather be.

The meal Rob prepared was excellent. Anne put down her fork and sighed.

"You're a good cook, Rob. That was delicious—and I can see I'm not alone in my opinion." Rob was feeding bits of leftover food to the cat and dog, who sat haunch to haunch beside his chair. Blue gulped his share, while Big Red ate with typical feline delicacy. "Didn't your mother ever tell you not to feed the animals at the table?"

He turned to her with a wide, almost boyish grin. "All the time."

Anne looked at him closely. "Why does the word 'long-suffering' suddenly come to mind when I think of your mother?"

His eyes crinkled with laughter. "She raised four children who take after their father when it comes to animals. It was all she could do to stop the house from being overrun with pets. Dad was always bringing some unwanted animal home. We had cats, kittens, dogs, rabbits, assorted rodents, a ferret named Farrah . . . and a raccoon. Rocky. He was our favorite."

Anne glanced at the cat and dog, chuckling at their hopeful expressions. "You've obviously learned restraint."

"Oh, I think the place will fill up eventually. I'm having a pond dug in the fall, out behind the barn. I was thinking of getting some water fowl . . . geese maybe, a couple of domestic mallards."

" 'Donald' and 'Daisy,' I suppose."

He sat back in his chair with a smile. "I was thinking of 'Aque' and 'Via'—Duck, of course."

Anne groaned and shook her head. "And I thought naming a red dog 'Blue' was bad." She grinned suddenly. "You could always call one 'Con.' "

His eyes sparked with amusement. "How about 'In' or 'Dee'?"

Anne started to giggle. " 'Dee Duck'—that's bad, Rob. Really bad."

"I could always get a goat and name him—"

Anne held up her hands. "Enough already!" Her eyes were soft with laughter.

"I was going to say 'Ralph.' "

"Sure you were." Anne stood and began stacking dishes. "Let's get things cleared up before this gets out of hand. You've got a dishwasher, I hope." She caught his eye as she reached for his plate, and started to laugh. "I can just see this place in a couple of years—overrun by animals with strange names."

He was smiling as he got up to help her take the dishes into the house and Anne realized how much it meant to her to see him smile, to see the sadness chased from his eyes.

"THERE'S A STORM COMING," Rob said. They were sitting on the riverbank, gazing down on the water and over the fields stretching out from the opposite shore.

Anne looked to the south, where thick clouds were massing. In the distance, gray streaks of rain trailed to earth, while lightning cracked the sky. "I hope it's a good one. I haven't seen a real thunderstorm in years."

His eyes were gently teasing. "You don't run and hide under the bed?"

"Never. I love storms. They're so exhilarating." She lifted her head and shook her hair back, feeling the rising wind skim cool, moisture-laden fingers across her face. Her eyes were half-closed as she took a deep breath, anticipating the lash of rain against her heated skin.

She felt sensuous and desiring, wanting badly to turn to the man beside her, to melt in his arms as his mouth found hers in a kiss she knew would engulf her with a passion she had never known before. Did she dare let him see what she was feeling?

"We should get back to the house," Rob said, getting to his feet. "That storm is going to hit any minute now." He held out a hand to her.

Anne slowly put her hand in his. Electricity jolted through her arm as his fingers closed around hers. He pulled her to her feet, and she stood close to him. Desire shone in her eyes, made her body taut and longing to yield. The tip of her tongue darted to moisten her dry lips.

Rob's eyes fastened on those pink, pouting lips and he pulled her closer, releasing her hand to clasp her shoulders. "Anne, I—"

She stopped his words with her mouth. White-hot passion stabbed her loins as he growled deep in his throat and closed his arms tight around her. She melted against the thrust of his body, clinging to him with the weakness of intense desire.

The kiss ended as thunder cracked threateningly above them. Simultaneously they looked into the darkened sky, then at each other. Laughing, they began to run toward the house, chased by the stinging lash of driving rain. Lightning followed, splitting the clouds with angry flashes. Thunder resounded with a rolling roar.

Breathless, Anne stopped just before the house, turning to look back on the storm. Rain pelted her, streaming down her face and plastering her dress to her body. Rob caught her shoulders in his hands and turned her around. Dropping his hands to her waist, he lifted her, laughing up into her face, then lowered her slowly, letting her body slide against his. Heat grew where their wet bodies touched, and when their lips met again, passion exploded with an intensity that matched the storm around them. Taking her hand in his, he led her into the house.

Rob closed the bedroom door, then turned to take her into his arms, capturing her lips again in a slow kiss of sensual exploration. Shivering with desire, she clung to him until he pushed gently away.

"You're chilled." His voice was low and husky as he thumbed wet hair from her forehead. He kissed her again, then his lips left hers reluctantly. "I'll get a towel."

Anne stood in the middle of the room, rubbing her hands over her arms, trying to clear her jumbled thoughts. Outside, the splash of rain slowed, then died.

Anne wanted Rob, longed for him to ease the ache of desire pounding through her. It would be so easy to make love with him . . . but was she emotionally ready to take that step? Just as important, was he?

Rob returned from the bathroom, towel in hand. He saw the troubled light clouding her eyes. "You're having second thoughts," he stated.

Anne nodded slowly, watching his face. "You are, too, aren't you, Rob?"

He let out a sharp breath. His eyes flickered to the picture on the dresser near his bed and then back at her. He reached out and lightly ran a finger down her damp cheek.

"On one level, no," he said, his topaz eyes glistening as they swept over her, but she saw the darkness in their depths.

Drawing away from him, Anne wrapped her arms tightly against her chest. It was all she could do to keep suppressing the physical urgency his kisses had ignited, but she knew she needed more than that from him. She had been right to stop before they had gone any further. With a tight, apologetic smile, she walked away from him, shutting the bathroom door behind her.

She had seen him look at the picture beside the bed. She didn't need to see the faces in the photo . . . she knew who they were.

How horrible it would have been if they'd made love and she'd looked up to see the smiling faces of his wife and child. How much worse it would have been for him.

With a weary sigh, Anne picked up a towel and rubbed it across her face, then began to dry her wet hair.

As she left the bathroom, she could see Rob through the windows, sitting on the railing of the balcony, hands clasped around one knee as the other leg dangled over the edge. He was gazing out over the river and Anne wondered what she would see in his eyes now that his passion had cooled.

Biting her lower lip nervously, she went outside.

He turned to her as she came through the glass doors. His lips attempted a smile that didn't lighten the bleakness that had settled in his eyes.

Her own smile was forced and she looked away from him, leaning against the railing. The storm had rolled on across the land. Moisture lingered in the air, but the wind had died to a cool breeze laden with the scent of washed earth. Patches of mist caught in the reeds along the river, where a great blue heron stood still and waiting.

"Anne..."

She turned to him. He held a hand out to her and she slipped her fingers through his. Without the glaze of passion, his face was still and unsettling.

As his thumb stroked circles on hers, Anne pushed aside her own feelings and smiled with gentle understanding.

"Tell me about her, Rob."

Rob took a deep breath and looked away. "She was a wonderful woman...vibrant and full of life. We were married for nine years—good years." He looked at her, his eyes dulled with sorrow. "I loved her, Anne. I never wanted anyone else."

She felt his pain. Tears welled in her eyes and she squeezed his hand in sympathy.

"Part of me—part of me died with Lisa and Jamie. I don't think I could ever feel that way about anyone again." He looked down on their clasped hands.

"You're a beautiful, passionate woman, Anne, and part of me needs that. But..." He raised his head and searched her face closely. "It wouldn't have been just sex, would it? Not for you?"

She shook her head, her breath catching on a sob as tears slid down her face. "I love you, Rob," she whispered. She couldn't pretend otherwise.

He pulled her to him, cupping her head to his shoulder as he rubbed his chin across the top of her head. "I'm sorry, Anne."

Anne pushed back, releasing her hand from his. "I should be going," she said, attempting to smile as she wiped the tears from her cheeks.

He frowned. "There's no need for you to leave."

Her face showed her regret. "I think there is." Staying could only make things worse for her. She hurt enough already. She turned to go.

"Anne, wait—"

He got up as she turned back to him and caught her in his arms, hugging her tight. "I'm sorry, sweetheart," he murmured against her hair. "I don't mean to hurt you."

"I know, Rob," she said, rubbing her cheek against his chest. "I guess it just wasn't meant to be." She raised her head and met his lips in a soft kiss, pulling away before it could become lingering... searching.

"Goodbye, Rob." She turned and walked away as new tears scalded her cheeks.

ANNE DID LITTLE the next day but try to cope with a hollow sense of loss. She had been hopeful, in spite of Judy's cautioning and her own wariness, that Rob would someday come to love her. But last night had shown her that while Rob might be attracted to her, he wasn't ready to start again.

He was still caught in the past, bound by a love that reached beyond the grave.

As the day lengthened toward evening, Anne began to wonder if maybe she was putting herself through a lot of unnecessary agony. She had left because it had hurt to realize he couldn't return her love, not because he'd asked her to. In fact, he'd wanted her to stay. Maybe she had been hasty. There was no reason they couldn't keep seeing each other.

It was almost dark by the time Anne made up her mind. Avoiding Rob wasn't going to make things better, not for either of them. Their talk had cleared things between them; they both knew where they stood. If all there could be between them just now was friendship, then so be it. It was far better than nothing. Feeling calmer once her decision was made, she started off toward his place.

Rob's house was dark except for a dim light in the living room. Anne stood for a moment in front of the open glass doors off the patio. Classical music came softly through the screen and she listened for a moment, strengthening her resolve. She tapped lightly on the glass, and then again when there was no answer.

Maybe he can't hear me over the music, she thought, and peered into the room through the screen. She could see little in the dim light, no sign of Rob. Tentatively she slid open the screen and stepped inside.

"Rob?" she called softly. There was no reply. She moved farther into the room.

Rob lay on the couch, one arm over his eyes, his head turned away from her.

"Rob, it's me." He made no reply and Anne crept closer. She saw the half-empty bottle of Scotch on the table beside him. A glass lay on its side on the floor, ice cubes melting on the carpet.

Photo albums lay scattered on the rug in front of the hearth. Anne glanced at them and then at Rob, her heart contracting in pity. She knew what she would find between the pages of those albums.

Maybe she hadn't been able to bring herself to examine the picture beside his bed, but she would look now. She sat down on the raised hearth and reached for an album, resting it on her knees for a moment as she looked at Rob. Music from the stereo softly filled the room with a hauntingly beautiful melody. Did the music hold memories for him, too? Slowly she turned the pages, exposing Rob's past.

His skill with a camera was obvious. Anne examined the clear, well-taken pictures closely, giving vent to her curiosity. Lisa was dark haired and pretty, her gray-green eyes sparkling vivaciously. And Jamie... Anne's eyes filled with tears as she looked at Rob's son.

Jamie was a sturdy toddler with a tumble of reddish curls and golden eyes that glimmered with mischief as he grinned, not for the camera but for the man behind it.

Love was evident in those pictures. They told Anne more than anything how much Rob had lost. Tears streamed down her face as she closed the album. Would he ever be able to say goodbye to them? Would the day come when he would want her love and be able to return it?

Anne went to kneel beside the couch, laying a gentle hand on Rob's arm. He muttered a sigh and turned, hunching his shoulders as he crossed his arms over his chest. Even in sleep, his face seemed set and brooding. She stroked his hair lightly, feeling an overwhelming rush of tender love, and she longed to take him into her arms, to soothe his pain and ease his sadness.

But she knew he wouldn't want that. His grief was private. If she really loved him, she would leave him alone, give him the time he needed to come to terms with his loss. With a shaky sigh she stood up, wiping the tears from her face. After a last, lingering look at the face that had become so dear to her, she left.

CHAPTER NINE

NUMB WAS A WORD Anne would have chosen to describe how she felt. *Helpless* was another. Her life seemed to have been put on hold. Part of her despaired that Rob would ever come to her free of his past, but hope refused to die. There was a chance, given time, that he might want her love.

But how long would it take? It wasn't hard for her to imagine what it must be like for him. If it had been her losing Rob... She shuddered, knowing the pain that would bring. She wondered if she would ever be able to love again.

Summer drifted into August. Anne saw nothing of Rob except for brief glimpses of his truck as he drove past her grandmother's house on his way into town. She knew it was probably better that way, yet she ached for his company.

She began to wish they had never shared those kisses. That taste of passion had sent them beyond simple friendship. She couldn't go further without his love...and he didn't love her.

Ken and Margo were due back within a week. Ken called from Rome to say they would spend a couple of days with Margo's parents before returning home with the boys. Anne's parents would be home the week following that.

With nothing but time on her hands, Anne concentrated on getting her grandmother's house ready. Her heart wasn't in the painting and wallpapering, but they kept her busy and tired enough to fall asleep at night.

She struggled in the heat late one afternoon to finish papering around the kitchen cupboards. The sky outside darkened with an approaching storm and she turned on the lights before she cut and hung the last strip of wallpaper. She was cleaning up when the first raindrops splattered against the screens on the open windows and she quickly closed them, trapping hot air inside the house. Flicking off the lights, she went outside, intending to dash up to the main house.

One look at the sky told her it would be best to wait out the storm. Dark gray clouds with a greenish cast swirled overhead. Blue-white lightning crackled, followed instantly by earsplitting thunder. Trees hit by violent gusts of wind bent like saplings and the cottonwood in the front yard groaned against the onslaught.

Anne stood in a sheltered corner on the veranda, watching with fascination, awed by the power unleashed by nature. Rain fell in big, splattering drops that became a deluge and the temperature dropped. Wind shook the house, rattling the windows in their frames. Lightning flared again, blindingly close, and Anne jumped, startled.

The crack that followed was more than thunder. It was a ripping sound, a shriek of protest over the fury of the storm. Severed by lightning, the cottonwood fell, the top half crashing down on the overhanging roof of the veranda before Anne could reach safety inside the house.

Thick, gnarled branches shattered the roof. Anne cried out in pain as a broken tip scored her arm in a deep, ragged gash. Blood welled, thick and red, diluting to pink as rain sluiced it down her arm. Before she could do more than stare in horror at the wound, a blow to her head sent her reeling and she clutched at the side of the house. Sobbing with pain, she slid down the wall and lay pressed against the wet, gray-painted floorboards, choking back a wave of nausea as the rest of the fallen tree crashed down around her, confining her with leafy green bars that creaked and groaned in the wind. Spots darted before her eyes, blurring to become a curtain of darkness. She slipped into unconsciousness.

SHE HEARD VOICES DIMLY, the words incomprehensible as she wavered in and out of consciousness. Frowning in concentration, she forced her eyes to flicker open, and she stared at the dappled shade surrounding her, trying to focus her attention.

"She's there all right, Archie." Rob forced his voice to be steady. "It's a real mess. We're not going to be able to get her out without cutting some of those branches away. Get up to the house and get the chain saw. And Archie—you'd better call for an ambulance. Hurry!"

He turned back to the wreckage before him, pushing in among the leafy branches as far as he could. "Anne! Answer me, Annie...."

He was able to reach an ankle and his fingers clamped on to the clammy skin. "Please, Anne—say something."

Anne heard the edge of desperation in his voice and she struggled to respond. Like being on the edge of a dream, she was aware of her surroundings but unable to move. She closed her eyes again and concentrated on the touch of his hand on her leg. With great effort, she forced his name through stiff, unwilling lips.

"Rob. I—I'm . . ." Her voice trailed off weakly.

His hand tightened and he let out a long breath. "We'll get you out of there—just hold on, Annie, hold on. It won't be long now." His fingers stroked her leg rhythmically, soothingly. "Tell me where you're hurt, lass."

It was still an effort to speak and she had to focus on each word. "My head . . . was hit. And . . . my arm . . . cut." She felt sleepy. Darkness beckoned warmly.

"I'm . . . tired," she said with a sigh.

"Stay with me, Anne. Talk to me. Come on, lass, open those eyes. You need to look at your arm. Is it bleeding? You can do it, sweetheart. You have to do it."

Struggling, Anne forced herself to obey. She was lying on the arm that had been cut, and as the distant, sick feeling began to fade, she became aware of a dull, throbbing pain. Rolling carefully onto her back, she squinted at the wound. Pressure from her weight against the floorboards had stopped most of the bleeding.

Rob's fingers stroked insistently. "Tell me, Anne—how is it?"

"Okay . . ." She could see him now, through the tangle of branches and the pieces of torn roof. His face was grim, pale beneath his tan. Her lips twitched as she attempted to smile reassuringly. "I'm okay."

It was true. She felt weak and somewhat disoriented, but the dizziness was fading. Her arm throbbed in tempo with her aching head, but nothing was broken. It could have been worse. Much worse. She could see now just how close the main trunk had come to crushing her. As it was, it trapped her with thick, caging limbs and broken boards from the roof. A shudder of claustrophobia coursed through her.

"Get me out of here, Rob," she pleaded shakily, feeling sick all over again.

"We're going to have to clear some of this mess away first, Anne. I sent Archie for a saw. He'll be back in a moment." Rob spoke gently, his fingers rubbing her leg in soothing circles.

He kept talking, insisting she respond, to keep her awake. He told her how he and Archie were on their way back from Carberry, how the intensity of the storm had forced them to pull over to the side of the road until it passed. When they were finally able to proceed, it had been Archie who had spotted the fallen tree, smashed into the side of the house.

Archie was back by the time Rob had finished the story, scurrying from the truck with a small yellow chain saw, his round brown eyes anxious.

"The ambulance is on its way, Boss. How is she?"

"Okay, I think. Cut up a bit, and shaken, but okay. Let's get her out of there." He took the saw and pulled on the cord. It responded with a sputter that turned into a roar.

The noise was almost more than Anne could bear. She pressed her hands against her ears as the saw ripped its way through the branches. The smell of the exhaust clogged her nostrils and she gagged as tears rolled down her face.

It was an immense relief when the saw finally stopped. As Rob pulled away the branches he had cut,

Anne pushed herself into a sitting position. Dizzy, she brought her knees up and rested her head against them.

Within moments, Rob was kneeling at her side. "Anne," he said urgently. "Look at me, Anne."

Anne did as he asked. "Ouch," she whispered, forcing a weak, watery smile.

He returned the smile, but his eyes were shadowed with worry as he looked at the raw, purple-edged cut on her arm. With gentle fingers he pushed aside her hair and probed at the lump he found just above her ear.

"Are you hurt anywhere else?"

Anne started to shake her head, but stopped with a wince of pain. "N-no."

"Then let's get you out of here." With a steadying arm around her shoulders, he helped her through the tangled mess of branches and shattered roof to where Archie was waiting, a blanket in his gnarled, work-worn hands. Rob took it from him and wrapped it around Anne.

"I need to lie down, Rob," she murmured, feeling dizzy and sick, leaning against him.

He scooped her into his arms and carried her to his truck, helping her to stretch out on the seat. As soon as she was prone, the dizziness passed, but the relentless throbbing ache remained in both her arm and head.

Rob stayed with her, sitting on the edge of the seat, next to her head. She couldn't see his face, but the touch of his hands as he stroked her hair was comforting.

"The ambulance just turned into the yard, Annie. Lie still while I go talk to them." Before he left, he pressed a warm kiss to the lines of pain cutting her forehead.

Before the ambulance left for the hospital, Rob assured Anne that he would follow just as soon as he dropped Archie off at home. She lay back against the crisp white sheets covering the stretcher and closed her eyes. Rob would be there for her.

X RAYS SHOWED no skull fracture. Anne's smaller cuts were swabbed with antiseptic. The gash on her arm was frozen, cleaned and carefully stitched. There was no pain, but she was sickeningly aware of every tug and pull of the needle. Nausea returned and she struggled to control it.

"Do I have to stay?" she asked the doctor when he had finished.

"You can leave if there's someone at home for you. Is there?"

Anne started to shake her head, when Rob pushed through the green curtain across the doorway to the cubicle.

"She can stay with me," he told the doctor. He stood beside Anne, taking her hand in his. "How is she?"

"There's a bit of concussion, aside from the lacerations. Nothing to worry about. You can wake her up periodically tonight, just to be sure she's okay, but as I said, there's nothing to worry about. She's okay." He smiled at Anne and patted her arm.

"Can she go now?" Rob asked.

"As soon as she's had a tetanus shot."

Anne gave a weak groan of protest. "Haven't I been through enough?" She hated needles.

The doctor looked at her over the top of his glasses and grinned. "You won't feel a thing."

"I've heard that before," she muttered, squeezing her eyes shut and turning away from the approaching needle.

The doctor chuckled. "What did I tell you?" he said to Rob. "She's feeling feisty already." He slid the needle into her arm and pushed the plunger. "There. Take her home and pamper her for a day or two." He helped Anne to sit up, and told her when to come back. "I'll take the stitches out then. And don't worry about scarring. I sew a fine seam and nothing much will show after a couple of months."

"Thank you, Doctor," Anne said.

"You're welcome." He turned in the doorway and looked at Rob, his dark brown eyes twinkling with laughter. "Try to keep her out of trouble, will you? This is the second visit this summer."

"I'll watch her like a hawk," Rob promised as the doctor left. He looked down on Anne, pushing the hair back from her face with his thumbs.

"Are you sure you're all right?" he asked, his eyes dark and brooding.

"I'm fine. Really. And Rob, if you'd rather, I can call Ju—"

He stopped her words with a scowl and a quick shake of his head. "Don't be ridiculous. You're staying with me." He picked her up in his arms and started to leave.

"I can walk," Anne protested without much spirit. She felt weaker than she wanted to admit.

Rob smiled crookedly, his eyes soft under the errant lock of russet hair. "Don't be ridiculous," he said again.

With a sigh, Anne wrapped her arms around his neck and pressed her face into his shoulder, taking comfort from his warm, familiar scent. It was wonderful to be held in his arms again.

ROB TOOK HER straight up to his room and set her on the bed. "I think you should rest for a couple of hours," he said. Turning from her, he rummaged in a dresser drawer and pulled out a sweat suit.

"Let's get you into this," he said, shaking out the folds. "Your clothes are still damp." His quick, nimble fingers unbuttoned her blouse and he gently eased it past the raw, black-stitched cut on her arm. He removed her bra and dropped the sweatshirt over her head with an efficiency that would have been impersonal but for the softness in his eyes, as he freed her hair and pushed it back from her face with gentle hands.

"Stand up for a second. We'll get you out of those shorts."

"I can do it," Anne murmured as she stood. She unzipped the shorts and rolled the damp, clinging denim down her thighs, then slipped quickly into the sweatpants Rob held out for her, fighting her embarrassment. Sitting back down on the edge of the bed, she looked at him, her blue eyes smoky with the remnants of pain and delayed reaction as she gave him a tired smile.

"Thanks, Rob. For everything."

"Just don't let it happen again," he said lightly. "Two rescues in one summer is about all I can handle. Now lie down and get some rest."

Obediently Anne slid under the covers. Rob sat on the edge of the bed, taking her hand in his.

"Feeling better?"

Anne nodded. Her arm and head still throbbed, but the fleecy warmth of Rob's sweat suit took away the chilled feeling and his attention made her feel secure and cared for.

"Good." He rubbed his thumb across her knuckles. "Can I get you anything—an aspirin, something to drink?"

"Not just now, thanks. I might need that aspirin later, though."

"Just let me know." He leaned down and kissed her lightly. "Get some rest now. I won't be far."

Anne watched through half-closed eyes as he left the room. Was his concern mainly a reaction to having found her in what could have been a disastrous situation? At the moment she really didn't care. His attention had left her warm inside, a welcome sensation after the bleakness she'd felt lately. She rubbed her cheek against the pillow, breathing in his faint, lingering scent. Then slowly she turned her head and looked at the top of the dresser. There was no picture. She stared for a moment, then her eyes blinked shut and she slept.

"ANNE. Wake up, Anne." Rob sat on the edge of the bed, shaking her gently.

With a little moan, Anne opened her eyes, then closed them again with a frown of pain. "My head hurts," she murmured. It throbbed as regularly as her heartbeat. So did her arm. She opened her eyes again and blinked at Rob. "What time is it?"

"A little after six. I made you a sandwich and some tea. Do you think you can manage it?"

"The tea, definitely." Anne carefully pushed herself into a sitting position, wincing as her stiffening muscles protested. Rob placed a pillow behind her and she leaned back against the headboard.

"How do you like your tea?" he asked, turning his attention to the tray he had placed on the night table beside the bed.

"With milk—and an aspirin."

He took a small bottle from the tray, and smiled at her as he opened it. "I thought you might need these," he said, shaking two tablets into the palm of his hand. He handed them to her along with a cup of tea.

Anne smiled gratefully and popped the pills into her mouth. She took a swallow of tea, sighing as the hot liquid eased the dryness in her throat. She took another drink. "Thank you, Rob."

"You're welcome. Now why don't you try the sandwich?" He took the plate from the tray and put it on her knees. "It's tomato—the first one from the garden."

Anne picked up half the sandwich and nibbled on a corner. She was hungrier than she'd thought, and finished the sandwich quickly. Rob poured her a second cup of tea, and as she sipped it, the pain in her head and arm receded.

"I feel a lot better now." She smiled her thanks.

Topaz eyes examined her closely. "You look better."

Anne gazed down at her cup and took a swallow of tea. Now that the crisis had passed and the shock was wearing off, she was beginning to feel self-conscious. She put the cup on the tray and tugged at the sweatshirt where it had slipped down over her shoulder.

"I could go home now," she ventured.

Rob frowned and shook his head. "The doctor didn't want you alone tonight. You're staying here. Now I've got a few things to take care of outside. Do you want to come downstairs, or stay and sleep some more?"

"I'll stay here." There were books and magazines on a night table. If she couldn't sleep, she would read. That way, Rob wouldn't feel obliged to entertain her. "And Rob—" she twisted the top sheet between her fingers "—I could stay in one of the other bedrooms."

"You're better off here. I'm supposed to wake you every couple of hours, remember? It'll be easier if we're in the same room." He grinned crookedly. "I think we could safely share a bed under the circumstances, don't you?"

Her lashes fanned flushed cheeks as she dropped her eyes and nodded. There was no danger of anything happening as long as she felt as fragile as she did. And why pretend? He knew she was in love with him.

Rob caught her chin between his thumb and forefinger, raising her head until he could smile into her eyes. "Get some rest, Annie," he said softly. "I'll see you later." He rubbed her bottom lip with his finger, then stood up and left the room with an abruptness that startled her.

Troubled, Anne slid down the pillow and lay quietly, staring into a corner of the room.

ANNE HAD NO RECOLLECTION of Rob getting into bed with her. What she did remember was how he had wakened her during the night, overriding her sleepy protests as he gently insisted that she talk to him for a moment or two. Once satisfied that she was coherent, he would let her drift off again. She also remembered the warm strength of his arms as he held her while she slept.

She was awake early, as she often was. Long, golden rays from the rising sun found their way through the screens on the open windows and trailed across the bed. Anne stretched cautiously, then examined the angry-looking welt on her arm with a grimace, deciding that the less she saw of the ugly black stitches the better. Her head was sore to the touch, but no longer ached.

Turning onto her side, she looked at Rob, his face relaxed in sleep. Unable to resist, she lightly rubbed a finger over the raspy stubble on his chin, then pushed back the hair that tumbled over his forehead. She caught his warm man-scent and she breathed deeply, her eyes half-closed with pleasure. For the moment, she was happy. . . content.

His eyes flickered open, caught hers. His smile was slow and sleepy. "How are you feeling?" he asked, his voice a husky whisper.

"A little stiff and sore, but otherwise much better." Warm and relaxed, feeling far less self-conscious than she would have thought possible, she let him pull her down until her head rested on his shoulder. He brought his arm up and held her to him, his fingers playing with the ends of her hair. She sighed and rubbed her cheek against his chest. *I love you so much,* she said to herself, wanting to say the words out loud, knowing she shouldn't.

The intimacy became almost overpowering, and Anne pushed away from him. "I need a shower," she said, struggling to keep her voice even.

Rob vetoed that idea with a quick shake of his head. "You might get dizzy and fall. You can have a bath if you watch those stitches. They have to be kept dry."

Anne sat up and frowned. "But I need to wash my hair," she objected, fingering a lock. "I can't do that in the tub."

Rob propped himself up on an elbow, watching her through narrowed eyes. "We'll manage." The look on his face told her he fully intended to supervise and she felt a flutter deep inside.

She pushed up her sleeves and said honestly, "Rob, I'm not going to feel comfortable having you in the room while I bathe."

"And I'm not about to let you in that tub unattended," he returned. "So cover up with a facecloth if you must—or do without the bath."

HER STITCHED ARM resting against the cool porcelain rim of the tub, Anne leaned back with a sigh of pleasure as warm water swirled around her. She had added a dollop of shampoo to the water and the bubbles made a foamy cover that hid most of her nakedness.

Rob came into the bathroom, carrying towels and a plastic measuring cup. "I'll wash your hair if you're ready."

Feeling a blush suffuse her skin, Anne sat up, bringing her arms up across her chest. She nodded, keeping her eyes down as he knelt beside the tub.

"Head back."

Closing her eyes, Anne tilted her head. Warm water cascaded down her back again and again as he soaked her hair. She felt the coldness of the shampoo touch her scalp and then his gentle fingers rubbing it in. Clean water from the tap in the sink rinsed the suds away.

"That should feel better." His voice was thick as he blotted her wet hair with a towel. Dropping the towel onto the floor, he picked up the bar of soap and began to wash her back.

Anne bit back a moan at the sensuous touch of his hands as they soaped from the small of her back to her neck and shoulders. She drew in a sharp breath when he reached around and cupped the weight of her breasts. Lubricated with soap, his thumbs drew circles around her nipples until they hardened and stood erect. He flicked them lightly, then moved over her ribs to her belly, then back again with torturous slowness. This time the moan escaped her lips.

The soapy caresses stopped. He picked up the cup again and used it to rinse the suds from her body. Then he pulled the plug and the water began to drain away. Her eyes dark with apprehension, Anne looked up to see him holding a towel out for her. She stepped carefully from the tub, looking quickly away from his eyes, feeling shy and very vulnerable. She would have reached for the towel to hide herself from him, but he stopped her with a shake of his head.

"Let me." His voice was deep with undertones of desire. Trembling, Anne stood there, wanting more of his intoxicating caresses.

He patted her face dry, pushing back the hair from her temples with a corner of the towel. Then he knelt in front of her, drying her feet and legs.

He looked up to see a droplet of water sparkling on the peak of her breast, ready to fall. Impatiently he flung the towel aside and reached for the droplet with his tongue. Anne's fingers raked through his hair and she pressed him closer, her legs trembling with hot waves of passion as she pushed against the bareness of his chest.

"Rob," she murmured. "Oh, Rob..." There was no fighting this.

With a growl of burgeoning desire, he stood up and swooped her into his arms, pushing through the doorway to the bedroom. Carefully he laid her on the bed. When she held her arms out to him, he took them and pressed them gently against the bed, his eyes smoldering as they looked into hers.

"Let me," he said again.

He pushed the wet hair back from her face and kissed her deeply. Then his mouth began a slow, searing downward journey, his teeth gently nipping, his tongue caressing. He relished the clutch of her fingers on his shoulders, the way she moaned in rhythm with the passion he felt surging through her. When at last he took her, she arched against him, aching with need. Her cry of appeasement mingled with the harshness of his breathing as he joined her release.

Anne lay relaxed against Rob, feeling his breathing deepen as he drifted into sleep. Carefully she moved his arm from her waist and slid out of bed, smiling softly as he rolled over with a murmur of protest. His black terry robe was draped across the foot of the bed and she put it on. It reached to her ankles and she tied the belt tight to prevent the shoulders from slipping down her arms. Picking up his comb from the dresser, she went outside to the deck.

It was late morning. Anne leaned on the railing, looking across the river as the sun warmed her back, and wondered what conclusions were to be drawn from the attention, the tenderness—the passion—Rob had shown her. Was he putting the past behind him, beginning to care for her as she cared for him? Anne frowned and gave her head a quick little shake. It would be wiser to assume nothing had really changed. Rob liked her and felt a physical attraction toward her. Nothing else was certain, and allowing false hopes to grow would only lead to more pain.

Sighing, Anne sat on a redwood stool, her back to the sun, and began the task of combing out her damp, tangled hair, careful to avoid the tender bump on the side of her head. Within moments her arm started to throb, and she stopped to rest it across her thighs, cupping a hand just below the cut.

Rob came out of the bedroom, dressed only in a pair of jogging shorts. Anne glanced at him sideways, her face partially hidden by a fall of hair; she smiled hesitantly as she watched for clues to what he was thinking.

"Is your arm bothering you?" he asked.

"It was fine until I tried combing my hair."

He smiled lazily as he pulled up a chair behind her. "I was worried that maybe you'd been a bit too—active this morning. Give me the comb," he said as he sat down.

Silently Anne handed him the comb, wishing she could see his face without having to turn around and look at him directly. She felt unsure in his presence this morning. There was so much she wanted to say, to ask, but the words simply wouldn't form.

Rob spread her hair until it fanned out against the black robe. He combed one lock at a time, watching as it dried into golden strands that felt like silk in his hands.

Anne felt the tension ease from her shoulders as she relaxed under his gentle touch. She gave her head a little shake and leaned back a bit, resting her arms on his thighs.

He raked his fingers through her hair, then lifted it to watch it cascade down her back. He lifted another handful and rubbed it against his face, breathing in the sun-heated scent. Dropping it again, he resumed the slow, rhythmic combing.

"Anne..."

His voice tightened and she tensed, wondering what he was going to say. She bit her lip and took a deep breath, strengthening herself.

"I've had a lot of things to sort through the past little while. It wasn't easy, coming to terms with how I felt about Lisa and Jamie...how I was starting to feel about you." He put down the comb and put his arms around her, resting his cheek against the top of her head.

Anne leaned against him, her eyes closed and her bottom lip caught between her teeth. Her heartbeat quickened almost painfully.

"It wasn't easy to say goodbye...Lisa and Jamie meant everything to me. And it was painful to realize—*really* realize—that all they can ever be to me now are memories. Part of me will always love them...but they're gone." He drew a deep breath and tightened his arms around her.

"When I saw that tree smashed against the house and knew you were under it...I thought I'd lost you, too, Anne. And just when it looked like it was too late, I knew how much you'd come to mean to me."

He took her shoulders and turned her until he could look into her face, smiling at the hope he saw there.

He kissed her gently. "I think I've fallen in love with you," he whispered.

Anne stroked the side of his face, her eyes large and luminous with emotion. "I hope you have, Rob. More than anything. But I don't want you to feel rushed or—or pressured into something you're not ready for."

As he started to speak, she laid a finger across his lips to stop him. "I love you," she said. "And for now, it's enough to know you might return that love. Just being with you makes me happy."

Rob held her close, gently rubbing her back as he breathed the sweet, clean scent of her sun-dried hair. "I feel like I've climbed out from the bottom of a cold, dark pit. You've warmed me, Anne, made me feel alive again. I want—I need—to be with you."

Anne rubbed her cheek against his chest, savoring the rush of hope and love that flowed through her. "Then I guess we're both exactly where we want to be, aren't we?" she asked serenely. Smiling, she looked up, meeting his kiss halfway.

"Ah, Anne," he breathed against her parted lips. "I'm so glad you came into my life. I love you—I know I do."

THEY WERE MARRIED in early October, the Friday night of the Thanksgiving weekend. They would have time for a flying visit to Rob's family before Anne's classes started.

It was a small, informal wedding held in the Hammond house. Anne wore a simple ivory-colored dress and matching jacket. She carried no bouquet, but pinned a delicate corsage of pink rosebuds to her jacket. Her hair was loose, the golden waves caught back with combs entwined with baby's breath. She smiled as she caught Rob's eye from across the room, thinking how different, how handsome he looked in his charcoal-gray suit. And soon he would be her husband.

They chatted with family and friends until the minister called them together. Hand in hand they faced him, Ken and Margo beside them as witnesses. Rob repeated his vows in a low voice filled with promise. Slipping a wide, gold band on her finger, he raised her hand to his lips, then pressed it above the steady thud of his heart.

Anne began to speak her vows, her soft voice tremulous as she saw the love glowing in his eyes. Nothing had ever sounded so right as the minister's words pronouncing them husband and wife. Tears sparkled in her eyes as she returned Rob's kiss of promise.

They slipped away from the party early. The autumn night was frosty clear and stars trembled in the inky sky. The air was sharp with the smell of dry leaves.

Rob had left the lights on in his house and it stood warm and welcoming in the dark night. As soon as the door shut behind them, Rob took her in his arms, cupping her head against his shoulder.

"Happy?" he murmured.

Anne sighed contentedly. "Completely." She raised her head and kissed him tenderly.

"Let's go upstairs," he whispered against her lips. "I've got champagne waiting." He took her hand and led up the stairs to his room.

"I'll change while you open the champagne," Anne said, picking up the small case she had left there earlier. Kissing him quickly, she went into the bathroom.

Rob was waiting for her when she returned; he was wearing his robe and holding crystal champagne glasses. He watched with loving eyes as she walked toward him.

She wore a flowing negligee of pale, shimmering pink. Released from the combs, her hair tumbled about her shoulders in silken waves. Her eyes glowed softly in a face flushed with happiness. Raising her hands, she pirouetted in front of him.

"Mother bought it for me."

"Thank you, Lillian," Rob murmured in approval. "You are very beautiful, Anne."

Anne's flush deepened and her eyes dropped from the intentness of his gaze. "Thank you, Rob." Looking up again, she smiled as she took a glass from him.

"To us," he said. "And to our love."

"And happiness," Anne added, touching her glass to his. She took a drink, then another one, savoring the taste against her tongue.

"More?" Rob asked.

She shook her head, handing him her glass. He put it down with his, then turned to her, holding out his arms.

"Come here," he commanded softly.

Willingly Anne went to him, wrapping her arms around his neck. Cupping his hands to the silk-wrapped curves of her hips, he pulled her to him as his lips found hers.

Her tongue flitted against the champagne taste of his mouth and she pushed her hands inside his robe, rubbing them over his chest. He answered with insistent caresses, pushing her back until he could nuzzle her breasts through the silkiness of her gown. As her nipples hardened, he nipped at them, wetting the material with his tongue until it lay translucent against her skin.

She whispered his name, her voice a plea. He swung her into his arms and laid her on the bed, stretching out beside her as his mouth found hers again.

IT WAS MUCH LATER when Anne sat cross-legged on the bed, the tangled sheet partially covering her. She looked at Rob lying back against the pillows, his arms behind his head.

"Rob," she said suddenly. "Are you happy? Really happy?" She watched him intently.

Rob reached out and drew her near. "Haven't I convinced you yet?" he asked huskily, rubbing a hand over her arm. "You make me happy, Anne. Very happy."

Anne sighed and nestled against his side. "I'm glad," she said with the contentment of security. "Rob..."

"Now what?"

She pushed back a bit and looked at him. "When... how long do you want to wait to have children?"

He caught a lock of her hair in his hand and tugged gently until her lips were close to his, then kissed her softly. "To be honest, I don't want to wait at all. I can't wait to hold our children in my arms."

Tears glistened in her eyes. "Oh, Rob," she whispered. "Can we start now—right now?"

His eyes darkened with emotion as he ran a hand down her side and pulled her close. "We can, Annie. We can."

INDULGE A LITTLE SWEEPSTAKES

OFFICIAL RULES

SWEEPSTAKES RULES AND REGULATIONS. NO PURCHASE NECESSARY.

1. NO PURCHASE NECESSARY. To enter complete the official entry form and return with the invoice in the envelope provided. Or you may enter by printing your name, complete address and your daytime phone number on a 3 x 5 piece of paper. Include with your entry the hand printed words "Indulge A Little Sweepstakes." Mail your entry to: Indulge A Little Sweepstakes, P.O. Box 1397, Buffalo, NY 14269-1397. No mechanically reproduced entries accepted. Not responsible for late, lost, misdirected mail, or printing errors.

2. Three winners, one per month (Sept. 30, 1989, October 31, 1989 and November 30, 1989), will be selected in random drawings. All entries received prior to the drawing date will be eligible for that month's prize. This sweepstakes is under the supervision of MARDEN-KANE, INC. an independent judging organization whose decisions are final and binding. Winners will be notified by telephone and may be required to execute an affidavit of eligibility and release which must be returned within 14 days, or an alternate winner will be selected.

3. Prizes: 1st Grand Prize (1) a trip for two to Disneyworld in Orlando, Florida. Trip includes round trip air transportation, hotel accommodations for seven days and six nights, plus up to $700 expense money (ARV $3,500). 2nd Grand Prize (1) a seven-night Chandris Caribbean Cruise for two includes transportation from nearest major airport, accommodations, meals plus up to $1,000 in expense money (ARV $4,300). 3rd Grand Prize (1) a ten-day Hawaiian holiday for two includes round trip air transportation for two, hotel accommodations, sightseeing, plus up to $1,200 in spending money (ARV $7,700). All trips subject to availability and must be taken as outlined on the entry form.

4. Sweepstakes open to residents of the U.S. and Canada 18 years or older except employees and the families of Torstar Corp., its affiliates, subsidiaries and Marden-Kane, Inc. and all other agencies and persons connected with conducting this sweepstakes. All Federal, State and local laws and regulations apply. Void wherever prohibited or restricted by law. Taxes, if any are the sole responsibility of the prize winners. Canadian winners will be required to answer a skill testing question. Winners consent to the use of their name, photograph and/or likeness for publicity purposes without additional compensation.

5. For a list of prize winners, send a stamped, self-addressed envelope to Indulge A Little Sweepstakes Winners, P.O. Box 701, Sayreville, NJ 08871.

DL-SWPS

INDULGE A LITTLE SWEEPSTAKES

OFFICIAL RULES

SWEEPSTAKES RULES AND REGULATIONS. NO PURCHASE NECESSARY.

1. NO PURCHASE NECESSARY. To enter complete the official entry form and return with the invoice in the envelope provided. Or you may enter by printing your name, complete address and your daytime phone number on a 3 x 5 piece of paper. Include with your entry the hand printed words "Indulge A Little Sweepstakes." Mail your entry to: Indulge A Little Sweepstakes, P.O. Box 1397, Buffalo, NY 14269-1397. No mechanically reproduced entries accepted. Not responsible for late, lost, misdirected mail, or printing errors.

2. Three winners, one per month (Sept. 30, 1989, October 31, 1989 and November 30, 1989), will be selected in random drawings. All entries received prior to the drawing date will be eligible for that month's prize. This sweepstakes is under the supervision of MARDEN-KANE, INC. an independent judging organization whose decisions are final and binding. Winners will be notified by telephone and may be required to execute an affidavit of eligibility and release which must be returned within 14 days, or an alternate winner will be selected.

3. Prizes: 1st Grand Prize (1) a trip for two to Disneyworld in Orlando, Florida. Trip includes round trip air transportation, hotel accommodations for seven days and six nights, plus up to $700 expense money (ARV $3,500). 2nd Grand Prize (1) a seven-night Chandris Caribbean Cruise for two includes transportation from nearest major airport, accommodations, meals plus up to $1,000 in expense money (ARV $4,300). 3rd Grand Prize (1) a ten-day Hawaiian holiday for two includes round trip air transportation for two, hotel accommodations, sightseeing, plus up to $1,200 in spending money (ARV $7,700). All trips subject to availability and must be taken as outlined on the entry form.

4. Sweepstakes open to residents of the U.S. and Canada 18 years or older except employees and the families of Torstar Corp., its affiliates, subsidiaries and Marden-Kane, Inc. and all other agencies and persons connected with conducting this sweepstakes. All Federal, State and local laws and regulations apply. Void wherever prohibited or restricted by law. Taxes, if any are the sole responsibility of the prize winners. Canadian winners will be required to answer a skill testing question. Winners consent to the use of their name, photograph and/or likeness for publicity purposes without additional compensation.

5. For a list of prize winners, send a stamped, self-addressed envelope to Indulge A Little Sweepstakes Winners, P.O. Box 701, Sayreville, NJ 08871.

© 1989 HARLEQUIN ENTERPRISES LTD.

DL-SWPS

INDULGE A LITTLE—WIN A LOT!

Summer of '89 Subscribers-Only Sweepstakes

OFFICIAL ENTRY FORM

This entry must be received by: October 31, 1989
This month's winner will be notified by: Nov. 7, 1989
Trip must be taken between: Dec. 7, 1989–April 7, 1990
(depending on sailing schedule)

YES, I want to win the Caribbean cruise vacation for two! I understand the prize includes round-trip airfare, a one-week cruise including private cabin and all meals, and a daily allowance as revealed on the "Wallet" scratch-off card.

Name______________________________

Address______________________________

City__________ State/Prov.______ Zip/Postal Code______

Daytime phone number____________________
Area code

Return entries with invoice in envelope provided. Each book in this shipment has two entry coupons—and the more coupons you enter, the better your chances of winning!

DINDL-2

INDULGE A LITTLE—WIN A LOT!

Summer of '89 Subscribers-Only Sweepstakes

OFFICIAL ENTRY FORM

This entry must be received by: October 31, 1989
This month's winner will be notified by: Nov. 7, 1989
Trip must be taken between: Dec. 7, 1989–April 7, 1990
(depending on sailing schedule)

YES, I want to win the Caribbean cruise vacation for two! I understand the prize includes round-trip airfare, a one-week cruise including private cabin and all meals, and a daily allowance as revealed on the "Wallet" scratch-off card.

Name______________________________

Address______________________________

City__________ State/Prov.______ Zip/Postal Code______

Daytime phone number____________________
Area code

Return entries with invoice in envelope provided. Each book in this shipment has two entry coupons—and the more coupons you enter, the better your chances of winning!

© 1989 HARLEQUIN ENTERPRISES LTD.

DINDL-2